The

Dead

Husband

Project

SARAH MEEHAN SIRK

ANCHOR CANADA

Anchor Canada and colophon are registered trademarks of Penguin Random House Canada Limited.

Library and Archives Canada Cataloguing in Publication

Sirk, Sarah Meehan, author
    The dead husband project / Sarah Meehan Sirk.

Short stories.
Issued in print and electronic formats.
ISBN 978-0-385-68760-7 (softcover).—ISBN 978-0-385-68761-4 (EPUB)

    I. Title.

PS8626.E3576D43 2017   C813'.6   C2017-900517-0
                                           C2017-900518-9

Cover design: Jennifer Griffiths
Cover image: *Still Life with Flowers and a Watch*, Abraham Mignon, c. 1660–c. 1679, Dupper Wzn. Bequest, Dordrecht

Printed and bound in the USA

Published in Canada by Anchor Canada,
a division of Penguin Random House Canada Limited

www.penguinrandomhouse.ca

10 9 8 7 6 5 4 3 2 1

Penguin
Random House
ANCHOR CANADA

To my mother and father

CONTENTS

THE DEAD HUSBAND PROJECT

Sweaty, limbs entwined, blankets kicked to the floor.

Paris.

Maureen Davis had married Joe McGovern five days earlier in a gown she'd made herself and pinned with flowers that had wilted before midnight. The ceremony bare in an unadorned gallery, the guests unsure whether it was real or performance art or something else altogether until the wine came out and the mini spanakopitas were passed around and Phil dumped a pile of blow on the altar, and then no one seemed to care one way or another. She'd been buoyant that night, her feet hovering inches off the ground as she bobbed along at her new husband's side through the riotous guests and the churchy scent of burned-out candles.

Joe rubbed his bare foot against the arch of hers. She shimmied closer over the sheets and pressed her back against him; he wrapped his arm around her waist. They were sticky and hot and smelled of fermented wine and smoky hair and they couldn't get close enough to each other.

"Everything enmeshed," he said, kissing the back of her neck. "Eating, working. Fucking, sleeping. Everything together."

Noise from the narrow cobblestone street below wafted up through the heavy, shifting curtains: male voices barking in rapid French, café chairs scraped along time-worn stones, laughter at the expense of someone. Impossible to tell if it was day or night.

"You say that now."

"Now. Always." He reached for a cigarette and lit it. "Forever and ever, amen."

He sat up and clicked on the radio, the ladder of his vertebrae pressing through his freckled back. Something unknowable beneath the surface. But she knew, knew each bend and curve and divot and mole. She traced her finger down the lowest part of his spine.

He took a long drag. "I've been thinking," he said. "I've got this idea. It would be collaborative."

He passed her the cigarette. His hair was flattened to his skull in parts, sticking up in others. Everything he did made him think. Everything he did made him want to create. Red creases from the sheets crisscrossed between the moles on his shoulder blades. She could feel his excitement, the heat of it. A furnace roaring to life. He was always coming up with new concepts, brilliant concepts. More now, it seemed, and she liked to think that she was his muse.

She took a drag and gave it back to him, rolling onto her stomach. She knew whatever it was would take him away, for a time. But that was who he was. And he was hers.

"What time do you think it is?" she asked, faking a yawn.

"Eight-thirty. The announcer just said it. *Vingt heures et demie.*"

"Oh. I wasn't listening." She was. Her French sucked. "We should eat something."

Joe stood, dropped the butt into a glass of water and swivelled his hips so his penis circled around and around. He kissed her before going to the bathroom to pee.

"It's that 'until death do us part' line," he said over the tinkle of his urine in the toilet bowl. "I've been thinking about what that means. Like, imagine if when one of us died, the other one—"

The rest of his sentence got lost in the flush, the blast of water in the sink. He gasped as he splashed his face.

She watched him sashay to the window and throw open the curtains to the Paris night, naked, his body stretched out like a star. Hoots and whistles up from the street, a woman shouting a cascade of incomprehensible words.

"I don't want to think about you dying," Maureen said.

He turned his face to her with his arms and legs still splayed, framed by the window. His expression draining of performance, his eyes quieting. He looked back out onto the street and over the rooftops.

"It's not about that." His voice almost tender. "It's about permanence. Love. What endures, what doesn't. What's left in the end."

He yanked the curtains closed and used his teeth to pull the cork out of the bottle of Bordeaux. "Anyway, it's just the start." He poured mouthfuls into each of their glasses. "Seeds. Nothing yet in the ground." He placed the bottle back on his nightstand, lit another cigarette and lay down beside her. "Decades to go before I sleep."

Miles, she thought. Miles to go.

She watched the smoke rise to the cracked ceiling, her hand searching for his in the wrinkled sheets. Such beauty in a crack, the patternless zigzagging of it, this scar of decay. The possibility that the floor above could give way and fall through, plaster and wood and frayed wires collapsing onto them mid-fuck.

She started to have ideas. Things falling apart often gave her ideas. He rolled on top of her, pressing her body into the soft mattress, blocking her view of the crack.

"Doesn't inspiration make you horny?" he asked. He took one last drag and dropped his cigarette into her wineglass.

—

Lilah Davis-McGovern can already picture the lineups. How the people will spill out onto the sidewalk and down the street, blocking doorways and winding around the corner where there's a bar with a patio. People idly shifting their weight, looking at their phones, making plans for later. She expects it'll still be warm enough to sit outside by then and she can see some girl there on the patio with her hair in a topknot, sipping on a pint of craft beer, lighting a menthol and leaning toward a guy in the lineup, saying, "Hey, what's going on?" Her face crooked with a smirk as she gestures with her cigarette toward the rest of the people waiting, the ones she can see on this part of the block. "New *Star Wars* movie out or something?"

The lineup guy will jab an index finger at his thick-framed glasses and look at her like she's from another fucking planet. He'll stare just long enough to establish his cultural superiority and say, "There's a dead body in the gallery around the corner. It's an installation."

The patio girl's eyes will open wide and spit will come out with her exhaled smoke.

"For real? You've got to be shitting me. Like, *dead* dead? That is seriously fucked up."

He'll nod and raise his eyebrows and return to reading old emails on his phone and she'll take another drag looking up and down the lineup at the asymmetrical haircuts and worn Converse and say, "So dead people are art now, huh?"

And he'll take a breath and almost launch into what he read about the piece in the reviews, how this signals the revival of Maureen Davis's long-dormant career and ignites pyrotechnics at the end of Joe McGovern's, but before he does he'll become aware of the people ahead of him who are listening now and who look like the types who actually know a thing or two about art, so he'll just say, "Yeah. I guess they are," in a voice he hopes sounds dismissive, bored and authoritative. He'll jab at his glasses again and squint at his phone but not without first glancing at the couple ahead to see the man smile at the woman because that was the right kind of answer to give to the kind of girl who doesn't know a thing about fucking art, and he'll feel good about himself as he takes a few steps forward along with the line.

"Lilah? Hon?" Joe gently prods her shin with his metal cane. "You coming?"

She looks around the oncology waiting room and sees Catherine, the nurse, standing by reception hugging files to her chest, her caked-on mascara framing blue LED eyes.

"Dr. Kadri's ready for you, Joe," Catherine says.

Lilah gets up and takes her father's arm. They shuffle their way behind Catherine, who's slowed her pace to match theirs, making it seem normal, as if she always walks that way.

Bernie steps away from Maureen to look out the window at the alleyway. "You're sure about this."

His office white, the floors dark maple and rubbed with beeswax. She swivels back and forth in the white moulded chair, plays with a postcard for the gallery's next show. *Vivi: all my yesterdays.* Vivi looks about twenty-one. How many yesterdays could she have? Maureen folds the corners down and sets it on the desk like a tiny table, then upends it like a helpless bug.

"Yes, we both are," she says. "It's been years, Bern."

He walks over to the slate counter to pour them more coffee.

She scrapes at nothing with her fingernail on his polished desktop.

He hands her back her mug thinking of her last show, a decade ago now, the tepid reviews, the remaining pieces now bubble-wrapped and boxed up on high shelves in the storage room beneath them.

"I'm sorry, Maureen. That you're going through this. I don't think I'd know how to be."

"That's just it," she says, putting her mug down on the bent postcard. "That's the point. It's about what happens in the aftermath. It'll put you right there. Beyond the grief, beyond the transition. You know, to what's left."

She's different. There's a spark about her, a lightness, a youth, despite the dark circles and red eyes. A hint of the old Maureen, just out of art school. She arranges her scarf like a sculpture around her neck. Her hands know how to move again. Sure of themselves, minds of their own. Artist's hands.

He flips through the sketches and plans in her portfolio. "What if you change your mind?"

"There are three versions," she says, pointing at the drawings in front of him. "Right now we're leaning toward the one without the Plexiglas. The one where we're in a kind of dance. But I'm still working things out with the Body Worlds guy. He's got to let me have more control of Joe's facial expression. If it doesn't happen, we can live with the encased version. That one," she says, nodding at the sketch of a man in a transparent box. "With Joe's hands on the glass? I just don't want people thinking 'Damien

Hirst' when they see it. Him, I mean. I don't want them thinking 'Oh yeah, the dead shark thing' and that's it." She rummages through her purse for her lip balm and smoothes it over her lips. Eucalyptus sharpens the air. "It can't just be the next iteration. It's got to blow out the fucking ceiling or there's no point."

She glances at her phone. Six missed calls.

"I agree," Bernie says, eyeing the drawing of Joe in a tank. He's thinking Hirst. He's thinking dead shark. "When do you hear back from Body Worlds? Anything I can do to get that—"

"I have to go," she says, tapping in her password. "I'll call you tonight." She grabs her jacket and purse and listens to her voicemail as she heads for the door.

"Maureen, I just think it would be more effective if—" He stops when he sees her slumped at the window. "Jesus," he says, going to her.

"Can I tweet this, Dad?"

"No."

"Come on. It's a fucking miracle."

"Language. Did you talk to your mom?"

"Tried her like ten times."

With Bernie, he knows. Her phone on silent in her purse; the plans, sketches, notes all laid out on the table in the gallery, ringed with coffee stains. They're probably making a list of who to invite. Editors, curators, major collectors. Firming up the artist's statement, deciding how to marry the funeral to the opening for maximum impact.

"Pass me your phone."

"Wait."

"If you tweet this you're grounded for a month."

"Easy there, Lazarus."

He goes to snatch it from her just as it rings, surprised at his own reawakened agility. Lilah ducks out of reach and answers.

"Mom! Can you believe this? We can't believe it!" She grins at her dad, eyes alight. "I'm totally shaking." Her words start firing like bullets from a semi-automatic. "It's like some kind of freaking miracle of modern medicine. You should have seen Dr. Kadri's face! He looked like he was in a fucking wind tunnel. Like he *obviously* didn't think Dad had a chance in hell. All that shit they said about the drug trial? They totally thought it would fail."

She looks up, passes him the phone. "Laz! Hey, Laz—I think Mom's in shock!"

Joe—

Maureen—

You must be—

I know. I know!

I can't believe . . .

Me neither.

Wow. I mean, just . . . wow. How do you feel?

I don't know. Alive? Alive! [*Laughs.*]

Alive, yeah. For sure. Alive. This is, wow, this is really something.

They'll keep testing but yeah. He says there's
nothing. It's gone.

But they're still testing.

They just can't believe it, I guess. But scan after
scan, nothing.

Nothing.

Nada.

Gone.

Yeah.

You okay?

Oh my God yeah! So much more than okay!

Yeah, I know, eh? I'm still just [*he exhales,
long and wavering*] just totally blown away.
Blown away.

Maureen takes a cab to get home before they do and goes
to her studio in the garage out back. She lights the roach
she'd left in the ashtray, takes a few pulls there in the quiet
beside the vase of wilting tulips, the cans of paintbrushes
and boxes of charcoal, the splattered, splintering easels
collapsed and leaning against the wall. Her hands are
shaking. She looks at the drawings of dead Joe taped
above her work table. The progression of the piece from
its conception, the earliest ideas sketched in Joe's own
renowned hand, to where she's got it now, nearly complete. She tears them down. They drift to the concrete
like fallen leaves. Detritus.

Soon the car will pull up in the laneway and park parallel to the garage door. She will hear Lilah's rat-a-tat voice

dip and crescendo with excitement like the little bird from *Peter and the Wolf*. They will expect to find her inside making a celebratory dinner. They will expect to see her face lit with relief. They will expect to have a cathartic family embrace wherein the pressure of the past few years will burst like a cyst and all the viscous grief and pain and fear will come oozing out.

She takes another pull off the roach, the heater searing her fingers.

The cyst breaks and something small and hard and sharp rolls out and clinks to the floor like a pebble, bouncing once on its way to the drain. The car pulls up. She's glad she'll have tears to show.

"I thought we'd just order pizza tonight," she calls out when she hears them on the other side. She presses the button and the garage door opens slowly, like it doesn't want to reveal too much too fast.

His old black Vans.

His shins like spindles in his jeans.

His faded denim shirt, loose, with sleeves rolled up. The crow tattoo on his forearm a smudge of black on loose skin.

His face grey, his eyes big and round and yellow and expectant.

She is holding the joint, adrift in a sea of dead Joes.

"Pizza sounds good," he says.

"Thank Christ." Lilah goes to help her father. "Does this mean we're done with that macrobiotic shit?" She closes his car door and places his hand on her shoulder for support.

"Amen," he says, leaning on her, and together they pass Maureen, scuffing and creasing the sketches underfoot as they make their way to the yard and into the house. The lights flick on.

Later that night, after Joe has vomited up most of his mushroom pizza and Maureen has helped him back to bed, she returns to the bathroom to sop up the mess with an old towel.

"I'm sorry," he says from the dark.

"Don't be. Not like I haven't done this before!"

He doesn't respond.

"Pizza was probably a bad idea. We should be easing you back into that kind of thing."

Asleep, she figures, when still she hears nothing.

"I'm sorry," he says again. Quieter now.

She uses the towel to scoop up the vomit and tosses it in the tub. While the water blasts from the faucet, chunks shooting up and smacking against the subway tiles, she wipes the remaining spatters from the floor with a facecloth, on her hands and knees, sobbing.

In the morning, sunlight through the blinds paints white bars on the walls and ceiling of their bedroom. He sleeps. Each of his breaths no longer a countdown; each of his breaths sucking air from the room. Maureen slips out of bed without disturbing the sheets, unhooks her robe from the back of the door and finds Lilah in the kitchen, at the stove, head bobbing to music from headphones.

She's making pancakes, singing tunelessly as she pours more batter into the pan, the stack beside her already way more than the three of them can eat.

It's not uncommon, Maureen wants to say. *It's not uncommon for there to be a surge of hope right near the end. A final little hill in the roller coaster before we speed down into the last dark tunnel.* Something she can add to her artist's statement. Yes, it makes sense, the more she thinks of it, that a vortex of emotion and attention and possibility would whip up around Joe at the end, ensuring maximum devastation upon his inevitable demise.

"*Hello?* Earth to Mom. I said, do you think Dad would like blueberries or chocolate chips in his?"

"Li, honey, I'm not sure if—"

"Tough call," Joe says, limping past with his cane. "Feels like a chocolate-chippity kind of day, don'tcha think?"

"Dad! I was going to surprise you!" Batter drips from her spatula as Lilah blocks her father from the stack. "This was supposed to be breakfast in bed."

"Careful—" Maureen lunges for the roll of paper towels to wipe up what spilled. "Careful. There are eggs in there. Bacteria." She throws the mess into the organics bin and washes her hands. Joe sprinkles more chocolate chips into the sizzling batter, licks his fingers.

"Dad!"

"I'm going to get the paper," Maureen announces, but Joe has Lilah in a fit of giggles. They don't turn when she goes.

Spring leaves shimmer in the breeze. Tinny reggae from an old Boombox on a porch down the way. A streetcar chimes the next block over and starlings chirp their panic from the top of every tree that lines the street. Maureen flops down on one of the weathered chairs and sifts through the paper to find the arts section, letting the rest of it slide down in a messy pile at her feet. A photo takes up nearly the whole first page. Vivi. Bernie's new artist.

A pull quote: *I went through a radical shift, like I was re-born. Everything was brand new. Everything.*

Vivi's hair is in a messy bun on top of her head, her jeans shredded and spattered with paint. She's smoking. She looks tired. She looks glorious. She's sitting on the floor in her studio, the long factory windowsill behind her lined with smooth stones and wildflowers.

The headline: "Youth Movement."

"Good morning!"

Maureen looks up. It's Rui, their grandfatherly Portuguese neighbour walking his terrier. She's now aware of her threadbare robe, her bare legs, her hair matted and greasy.

"Joe's going to live," she blurts out, as if to explain her state. "We found out yesterday."

"Oh how wonderful," he says, stopping. He looks genuinely relieved in the way that good, warm-hearted people can for someone they barely know. "That is just wonderful news."

"Some kind of freaking miracle of modern medicine!" Maureen yells, laughing. She cocks her head toward the door as if she's heard something. "Oh! Lilah's calling. We're having pancakes. It's a celebration. A pancake celebration!" She gets to her feet and begins to gather the paper together, the belt of her robe loosening.

"Well, God answered all our prayers," he says as the dog chews on some weeds. "Truly, truly wonderful news. I'm so happy for you all."

The breeze picks up, blowing sections of the paper around the porch and Maureen's robe wide open, her nightshirt beneath barely reaching the top of her thighs.

"Oh!" She tries to cover herself with one hand, grasping for the pages with the other. She sees Rui see the unshaved tuft between her legs. He presses his eyes shut and turns his head toward the street.

"Oops! Damn paper!" she says, forcing a chuckle and clutching at the flaps of her billowing robe as she scrambles, hunched over, around the porch. Finally able to wrap it around her, she knots the frayed belt tight enough to crush her abdominal organs, and snatches up the pages in a crumpled heap.

Rui yanks the leash to get his dog out of Maureen's garden and quickly starts on his way again.

"Well," he says, not looking back. "Well, please give my best to Joe."

She closes her eyes, cringing as she makes her way back through the house to the kitchen where she dumps the crinkled hill of weekend paper on the table.

"What the hell happened?" Lilah asks, clanking her syrup-streaked plate in the sink.

"Oh. Wind. It's windy."

Lilah begins to shuffle through the shifting wad. "Dad wants the arts section."

"Well, it's somewhere in there." Maureen tugs the belt tighter around her waist, making breathing near impossible, and takes a pancake off the remaining stack by the stove. "I'm going to go get some work done."

Lilah stops. Looks at her. "Are you for real?"

"Just for an hour or so. I need to finish up a couple of things."

Her daughter blinks. "You're joking, right?"

"No, I'm not *joking*, Lilah. I've got some things—"

"Newsflash: Dad's not dying."

"Lilah . . ." She thinks of what to say, but can only come up with: "That's enough."

Lilah shakes her head, returning to the paper. "I mean," she says under her breath, "the only thing that's dead is your stupid fucking installation."

"Lilah! I've had enough of your mouth."

Her daughter finds the arts section, flicks it in the air in front of her to iron out the creases, and glares at her mother on her way out of the room.

Her studio doesn't feel like a studio. It feels like a garage. She can almost smell the gasoline and cleaning solvents in the shadows and dusty light. Can almost see the metal shelves stacked with tools, old bicycles leaning against the wall, an oil stain on the ground beneath the fallen dead Joes. She gathers up the sketches for the recycling bin but stops herself. She lays them on the work table.

Maybe not now, she thinks, fingering the drawings of Joe in a box, Joe on a chair, Joe lying curled up on the ground, naked and fetal. Maybe not right now, maybe just a few more years. But it is cold comfort.

Her phone vibrates in the pocket of her robe.

Bernie.

He must have heard the news about his top-selling artist.

She had been on the verge. She'd felt it crowning. She could already see the front page of the arts section, the cover of *Artforum*. She'd practised her expression: the flat-line of a mouth, the volcanic eyes, the grief that was to be roiling under the surface. It was her turn.

"Stop," she says out loud, tears in her eyes. "Stop, you stupid, stupid child."

She should feel like a monster for thinking it. But fuck it if it wasn't true.

She lights a cigarette and opens the garage door, exhaling into the face of a girl passing by. "Oh shit." Maureen flutters her hand in the air to clear the smoke. "Christ. I'm so sorry."

The girl smiles, gives the peace sign. She's wearing oversized headphones and dark '80s Ray-Bans, her black hair roped in a braid down her back. Maureen watches her go, her mind morphing the girl into someone she couldn't possibly be.

Claudette.

Claudette at Joe's show some twenty years ago. Black hair, sunglasses, oracular smile. Stepping out of the gallery and onto the sidewalk where Maureen had escaped to get some air.

"You're Maureen Davis, aren't you?"

"I am, yeah. Joe's wife."

"I'd heard that," she said, putting her shades on her head. "Must be cool to live with another artist. I was going to say that I really loved your Woman Burning series. I was a couple of years behind you at OCA. Big fan. What are you working on now?"

"Oh. Well," Maureen started. She was rattled by the recognition. She wasn't working on anything. They'd been travelling; Joe's work stirring interest in New York, London, Düsseldorf. Paris. She'd wandered European streets while he met with dealers and curators and gallerists, drinking on her own in sidewalk cafés, studying the way people moved and talked in these foreign cities. Archiving it, she'd tell herself, for her own future work. "I'm at the embryonic stage with a couple of projects."

"I hear ya, I hear ya. Totally. I'm the same."

They stood watching the cabs and streetcars inch their way along, the city's edges softened by the setting sun. "Hey," Claudette said, leaning in. "I hope you don't mind me asking, but are you okay? You seem kind of sad."

Maureen felt something quake. "Oh, really? That's funny. I'm not. No. Not at all."

"Sorry." Claudette sidestepped closer, their arms now touching. "I've been drinking since noon. My radar's probably off."

She took out a pack of cigarettes and offered one to Maureen. They watched the traffic in silence, Claudette squinting each time she took a drag, lines appearing by her eyes that made her look older than she was. Her loose tank top fluttered in the warm breeze, hair escaping her braid in blowing wisps.

When she'd had enough, she flicked the butt into the street, orange sparks against the grey. She took Maureen's out of her mouth and flicked it too.

"Shall we?" She smiled, closer still.

Maureen followed her back into the gallery, past Joe who was listening to a major collector and his smiling, nodding wife ("Brilliant. Scathingly brilliant. They'll call you a misogynist but they just can't see what you're really trying to do here"), past the tight pack of young art group-ies with their wine in plastic cups and their giddy glances at Joe, past the larger-than-life installation of a woman being quartered by rabid wolves, down the narrow creaking stairway to the bathroom door. There wasn't much space for two at the base of the steps and when Claudette turned to touch her they were face to face. Maureen closed her eyes, surrendering to the tectonic shifts, to the shockwaves radiating from her core.

"Hey!"

It was Joe at the top of the stairs, glaring down at where they were pressed together.

"Hey! Get up here."

"Nothing happened," Maureen said in the back seat of the cab while he smoked out the window on the way home. She liked the way that sounded, like something could have. Like something did. She said it again. "Nothing happened."

He didn't say anything for a long time. After a few minutes he tossed out his cigarette and wiped his face with his hand, pulling at his eye sockets. "It's just that, I don't know, you can be so humiliating."

It was years before Maureen saw her again. Not until a talk at the AGO when one of Claudette's lauded light and audio installations was there after showing at the Venice Biennale. By then Claudette had relocated to Berlin and had pieces in the permanent collections of the Tate and MoMA, pieces, the reviewers effused, that had the power to break your heart. People would line up for hours in the rain, in the cold, in the stifling heat outside a gallery, waiting for their turn to step into her pulsing creation, put on the headset and fall to bits. Videos were made of them, arms outstretched, reaching for something that wasn't there, tears rolling down from under the boxy visualization goggles. They'd walk out, dabbing their eyes, murmuring to one another about her genius.

Lilah was three months old when the show came to Toronto. Maureen, deadened by sleep deprivation, strapped her in a baby carrier and waited in line all morning outside the gallery. But when she was next to go in, she turned away. She told the startled woman behind her that it was because she'd had her heart broken enough times and didn't have the energy to take it once more. They'd laughed together at the supposed truth of this. The woman cooed at Lilah.

Maureen wandered the other galleries, her mind soupy as she gently bounced along, hoping to get Lilah to fall asleep before Claudette's talk began. When the baby finally drifted off in front of an A. Y. Jackson, Maureen considered slumping into a chair to nod off herself, but instead bobbed her way to the auditorium and slipped into the shadows at the back where she could stand, rocking from side to side, without disturbing anyone.

Claudette sat cross-legged on a stool on the stage, a fringed scarf wrapped twice around her long neck, and took questions from the audience at the end. A young woman went up to the mic to long-windedly explain how her master's thesis pivoted on the heart-breaker piece at the Tate Modern, and specifically how it may or may not have been responsible for the otherwise inexplicable waves of (a) divorces and (b) dead birds that fell from the sky in the wake of its installation. Claudette smiled, awaiting her question. The young woman cleared her throat and asked, "What is the best piece of advice you've ever been given, as an artist?"

Claudette tittered, thought about it a moment.

"Let other people have babies," she said.

The audience erupted in laughter.

"Let other people get married!" she called out, taking a swig of bottled water as a second wave of hilarity rose up.

As if on cue, Lilah started to cry.

Shh, shh, shh, Maureen bobbed.

People in the back row turned, their faces lit with laughter, their attention now on Maureen and her strapped-on wailer as though they were part of the show. Row after row, others turned to look, their mirth reigniting. Claudette shielded her eyes against the spotlights, trying to see what was happening.

"There's a baby, a baby crying . . ." voices explained.

"Oh." Claudette nodded, took another swig. "I'm sure he's adorable."

Maureen curtsied good-naturedly at the ensuing eruption (the loudest yet), trotted out of the shadows and out the auditorium door. The squirming, red-faced, infuriated mass of a child began to catch her breath with the rhythm of her mother's fast-paced walk, and was asleep again by the time they reached the subway. Static crackled at the end of Maureen's nerves. Her breath shallow and quick. But at least she could stop bouncing; the subway provided enough movement and sound for them both as it clanked and shifted and rumbled its way under the streets.

She kissed the top of Lilah's warm head. She breathed her in. She closed her eyes for a brief standing nap. She decided to get off two stops early to pick up salmon and potatoes and olive oil and green beans for dinner. They could walk the rest of the way.

"Mom! Are you out there?"

Maureen tosses her cigarette into the laneway.

It's Joe, she thinks, her heart racing. He's collapsed. The pancakes, the chocolate chips, the pizza—it was all too much for his vulnerable system. The excitement, the good news. It pushed him over the final lip of life. This is it, she thinks as she darts back through the studio toward the house. This is it.

"I'm coming!" She runs up the crooked steps to the back door. "Li? Have you called an am—"

Music, coming from the street. Trombones, trumpets, the pound of a bass drum. It sounds like a marching band closing in. Lilah and Joe are on the front porch, leaning on one another, laughing. Joe is waving his cane out at the road.

"Mom! You have to see this!" Lilah reaches back for her mother's hand and pulls Maureen beside her.

Dozens of black helium balloons float above the heads of people she hasn't seen in years. White streamers trail from slow-moving stilt-walkers. A tattoo-covered man leaps ahead of the band and swallows an arrowhead of fire. A woman in a beard lugs a styrofoam cross as others fan her with palms. Someone's pulling a wagon and ringing a large bell, the passenger yelling in an exaggerated British accent, "I'm not dead yet!" And leading the way, in full zombie drag, are Don and Phil from Joe's former art collective.

The band reaches the front lawn and marches on the spot, still playing the tune ("Alive" by Pearl Jam, it dawns on Maureen) as the paraders let go of their balloons, launching a black plume of shifting constellations that get smaller and smaller and disappear much faster than anyone expects. Artists and writers and old friends line up to hug and kiss Joe on their way into the house, and within minutes the main floor is transformed. A DJ sets up his turntables on the dining room table, and big coolers of ice jammed with beer and cheap champagne are dumped on the kitchen floor.

"Did anyone bring OJ for mimosas?" someone calls out. "Or is it noon yet?"

A few remaining black balloons drift up to the high ceiling. An antique throne is carried into the living room and Joe is lifted onto it, a cold beer pressed into his hand. One after another, the paraders crouch at his knee and talk to him in earnest tones, laughing as they wipe tears from their faces. The band members take off their red-tasselled hats and jackets and strew themselves lazily across the lawn and the porch, the trumpet player leaning against the front door as he chats up Lilah, gesturing self-consciously with the beer bottle in his hand.

Maureen is still in her robe. She is cornered by Phil, who towers over her in his size 13 stilettos, his eyelids caked in sparkling green below a platinum Dolly Parton wig. The rest of his face is expertly contoured with grey and black makeup. He looks like he's been dead for days, but Maureen knows he's just come back from directing a Justin Timberlake video.

"You don't mind us sharing in the excitement, do you, hon? We had this all ready to go for Joe's funeral." He takes a long pull off his empty cigarette holder and blows pretend smoke in her face. His breath smells like stale mornings. "So much better this way, isn't it?" He smiles and turns on his heel, teeters delicately into the living room. He was one of the few people who knew what they had planned for Joe's body. He hated the idea. He called it gauche and told Joe that Maureen wasn't Marina Abramović. She could never pull it off.

She goes into the kitchen where the lights are now out and the window is covered with a blanket so people can dance in the dark with glow sticks. She saw Joe on his throne with a pink one encircling his thin neck. He looked like a target in a carnival game. Ten points! The dancers spill into the dining room and push the table-turned-DJ-booth to the wall on its squeaking casters. Down the hall, neighbours appear at the front door inquisitively; the revellers in the hallway encourage them inside. Maureen waves away plastic glass after plastic glass of champagne, pours herself coffee, and ducks around an ecstatic dancer to get milk from the fridge. Through the doorway she sees her neighbour Rui with his arm on the mantel, nodding to the music. Their eyes meet. He winks. She shudders.

All around her people are buzzing.

Oh, Maureen! You must be so happy! This is incredible! Come here, let me give you a hug! Oooooh—ooooooh!

Oh my gosh! Aren't you, like, his wife or something? This must be such a crazy mindfuck for you. Anyway, cheers!

People she knows and people she's never met squeeze her tight, her coffee sloshing over the rim of her mug. The house pulses with bass. Bernie appears at the front door, a small wonder of a girl trailing behind him. Vivi. Some of the people waiting to talk to Joe break away and swarm her. She's shaved her head and rimmed her eyes in purple.

Bernie, beaming, steps out of the way to witness her coronation from a proud and happy distance.

Maureen has an idea. She presses through the partiers to get her camera from the safe in the garage. She affixes a large flash, wraps the strap around her hand and wrist like a tensor bandage and makes her way back into the house. She starts in the dark kitchen.

The glow stick dancers are caught off guard. The cupboards brightening to a blinding white each time she shoots.

"Hey! What the fuck?"

The dancers cover their faces to block out the light or hold up their hands to get her to stop. She pushes her way into the hall, aiming the camera at face after flinching face, a contrail of blinking eyes in her wake. Vivi looks right at her with a tranquil smile.

"For the society pages!" Maureen shouts, laughing, shooting now like the paparazzi.

She elbows through the crowd in front of Joe and stops a few feet in front of him.

Flash.

Flash. Flash.

He raises his hands to shield his face. "Mo, what are you doing?"

Flash. Flash flash. Flash.

Still shooting, she holds the camera out in front of her. Her face blank.

"Maureen?"

He drops his hands and looks at her. He looks tired. He looks thin. He looks sick. He tries to communicate

something to her with his eyes in the way married people do.

Flash. Flash. Flash flash.

She has no idea what he's trying to tell her. They never
did have that ability.

Flash.

It's hard to know how long she's been at her laptop in the
garage, or how long he's been leaning against the door-
frame waiting for her to notice. The ashtray beside her a
mass grave for the pack of Belmonts she's smoked. She
extinguishes another, its remains tumbling on top of its
fallen kin.

"That's a good one," he says. "Good light."

She turns from the photo she's uploaded, a picture of
a shirtless guy with big, shocked eyes, people dancing with
glow sticks behind him. He looks naked.

Joe's shadow falls long from the doorway, reaching
almost all the way to the garage door. It's getting late. She
goes back to her computer, marks the image as one to
return to, and continues clicking through the photos.

"They're still going in there," he says, nodding back at
the throbbing house. "Unreal."

Click. Click. Click.

He takes a breath. "I'm really tired."

Click. Click.

She stops on a picture of Joe. His frozen eyes wide and
questioning, the harsh flash cutting deep shadows in the
pits of his cheeks.

"Jesus," he says, taking a step closer behind her.

She crops the shot tight around his face and hits Return. Hollows fill the screen.

"Okay, I can see you're busy."

She can tell from his voice that he's turned away.

His cane clacks against the concrete floor as he goes to leave. She closes her laptop. Some part of her wants to get up, to hold him, to rock together with him in their untended yard, but that part of her thumps from behind a wall built too long ago. She doesn't move from the stool.

He laughs suddenly. "You know, we talked about it a million times but I just couldn't get my head around it. The gone part. The utter obliteration of it. The *moonlessness* of that kind of night."

"That's very poetic."

He sighs, tapping his cane on the ground. "When did you become such a bitch?"

She lights another cigarette, relieved to feel something, even if it is rage. It dissipates only slightly when she hears his halting gait swishing through the grass back to the party.

"Mom? Mom, relax. It's okay. It's just me. Come to bed."

Maureen's neck is stiff and sore. Her arm numb. She has no idea where she is.

"You fell asleep in here." Lilah brushes hair out of her mother's eyes. "You missed a hell of a party. But it looks like you had a pretty good one in here on your own."

An empty bottle of expensive Napa cab sauvignon beside her. A full glass poured, untouched. She lifts her head, heavy with disappointment. She'd been saving it for a night when she had something to celebrate. Her lungs feel raw and scorched. On the laptop, the image of Joe she'd been digitally manipulating is pixellated beyond all humanity.

"Glad to see you're working on something new," Lilah says. "Looks pretty cool, actually."

There is that, at least.

The arm on which she'd been sleeping tingles as blood flows back to her fingers. She lets Lilah help her back to the house, where the stragglers are passing a joint on the front porch and flipping through her wedding album, their hooded eyes through the living room window only faintly curious as Lilah leads her mother down the hall and up the stairs. Maureen is still in her robe, and doesn't even have any socks to take off before she curls up like a shell on the bed.

There are more people here than she expected to see. Bernie smiles at her over the shoulder of a collector who's been hovering territorially by the hyper-pixellated photo of the stunned dancers with glow sticks.

"It's so meta," she overhears someone say, "the way she managed to capture the whole art scene like that? And just, like, totally deconstruct it."

The Resurrection of Joe McGovern, the show is called. Joe is leaning on his cane by the back wall, holding a glass of what must be now warm white wine as he nods politely and listens to a gesticulating critic in a felt fedora. She watches people pass him, look at him, uncertain of where he fits in all of this. He's standing by an image of himself that no one would know is him.

"So glad you went in this direction, Mo," Phil says. He still towers over her, even without his stilettos. He snatches a piece of sushi off the tray of a passing white-shirted server and pops it in his mouth. "Of course, you couldn't have done it without me." He winks. "Without me, without my party, there's no *you*." He blows her a kiss as he bows, retreating into the rest of the crowd.

Maureen doesn't have a chance to tell him to go fuck himself because he's already gone and there, beside her, is Vivi, who's saying she's been waiting for a chance to talk to her, and that she's always been a huge fan, and that she'd heard about her Woman Burning series, and that it'd been something of a legend among her peers.

"And honestly?" she gushes, gesturing at the walls around them with her wineglass. "Just coming up with this idea on the spot like that? With all you'd been through, with what must have been going through your mind that day? I mean, it's genius. Just brilliant. I'd love to talk to you about your process. Just, like, pick your brain."

Maureen nods, smiling faintly. She can't look her in the eye. This feels too easy. She looks around, bracing for someone to point it out, to call her a fake. If it had been Joe who'd done this he would have shrugged and called it "inspiration" and moved on to the next thing, the next piece, the next project, the next conversation without overthinking its genesis, without doubting himself, without looking back.

Was that was this was? Inspiration?

She sips her wine, scanning the room. The gallery assistant is putting yet another red dot beside a piece. They're almost all sold. People buying messed-up pictures of themselves.

"Can I get a shot of the happy couple?" asks a photographer from the *Globe*, ushering Joe over with a wave.

"Here, why don't I go over there," Maureen says. She puts her glass down and hurries over to her husband so Joe won't have to make the effort. She can't help feeling bad for him. She's not used to being the one in the spotlight. Maureen puts her arm around his waist. He keeps his hands on his cane. They smile.

Flash. Flash flash.

The photographer checks the image on the back of his camera, nods his thanks and turns away, candidly shooting the crowd.

"Well," Joe says. "Nice turnout."

"Yeah. I guess you never know with these things." She folds her arms over her chest, rubbing her bare biceps.

"Just glad I'm here to see it."

They laugh, together, but differently.

"I think I need to get some air," Maureen says after a moment.

He nods his head to the side, indicating she go without him. His smile means: I'm good, I'm okay. But he looks vulnerable.

"Go," he says when she hesitates, waving her off with his cane.

She manages to sneak out without being seen and finds a quiet patch of sidewalk in a shadow, the toes of her red Mary Janes poking over the edge of the curb. She tucks her lighter back into her cigarette pack and exhales into the warm night air, closing her eyes. The sounds of nighttime traffic wash over her. Baptismal.

"Mom?"

She turns. Lilah is jogging over. By the glint in her eyes it looks like she has good news. She looks so pretty with her hair down like that, bouncing off her shoulders in waves. Such light in her eyes.

"Mom—"

But Maureen doesn't hear what her daughter has to say. A cab swerves to avoid two guys who tumble, play-fighting, onto the street. The driver hops the curb, mowing Maureen down like a dandelion.

"Maureen," Joe says in a delicate whisper, just audible, as though she's made of the thinnest glass and anything louder would shatter her to sand. He's holding her hand. "Maureen, honey, it's me."

His eyes are bloodshot, lids heavy. She feels nauseated and tired and her head is splitting. There's an ache in her back that radiates along her ribs, making it hurt to breathe. Above her the lights glare an unblinking blue-whiteness at the walls, at the floor, in her eyes.

"Li—" she says. It's hard to make words. Her throat sore, her mouth dry as wool.

"Shh, no. Don't try to talk." He's leaning closer, stroking

her head. He kisses her hairline. "I'm just so glad you're here."

She goes to move her arm but can't bend it. It's in a cast. She tries to move other limbs and digits: her left leg is encased in rigid plaster too, as are her left hand and wrist, her torso immobilized by some kind of brace. She wiggles her toes. The scratch of bedsheets.

Someone coughs.

Shhhhh! A reprimand.

Slowly, slowly she turns her head. Beyond Joe, who's sitting on a wooden chair at her bedside, beyond the Plexiglas walls that surround them to make a room within a room, dozens of people are holding up their phones, recording her. A woman wipes away tears.

"I can't believe we're here for this!" someone hisses. "I can't believe she just happened to come out of it now—when we're here! This is *awesome*."

The people start clapping. Some are reluctant to put their phones away, they don't want to miss a second, so they slap the side of their legs with one hand while filming with the other. The applause picks up like rain hammering a tin roof, rattling across the room and out through the open door.

"She's awake—she just woke up!" people call to the lineup outside. Faces press against the front window of the gallery above a sign that says

THE VIGIL | JOE McGOVERN

Joe kisses her again. Whistles ripple through the crowd. Flashes now from cameras. She winces at the pain in her head and feels something cold on her chest. A woman in scrubs with a stethoscope smiles down at her, then checks the monitor beside them. The three of them enclosed in the Plexiglas room.

Maureen scans the walls. Her pieces are gone, replaced by sketches and paintings of a figure, sleeping or unconscious, hovering in space. In some drawings it's barely there at all, a faint outline only visible if you know where to look. Joe leans over her and closes his eyes as he touches his forehead to hers. She feels the pressure as he lets go, dozing, his head lolling to the side then jerking upright as he fights to stay awake.

"Welcome back, Maureen. I'm Dr. Fisher," the woman in scrubs says over the applause. She says Maureen had been in a coma for weeks. They didn't know if she'd ever recover. "But your vitals look great. Everything looks great."

Maureen wants to get up. She wants to get out of here. But she can't move, she can barely talk. She shuts her eyes against the cameras and the noise as the people shuffle their way around the room and back out the door, their time up. The next group presses in.

"Mom!"

She lifts her head as high as she can, an inch off the pillow. "Lilah?" she rasps.

"Mom?" Lilah kicks at the Plexiglas, nearly hysterical. It can't be opened from the outside, and Joe's fallen asleep, his head on the bed. Dr. Fisher squeezes around to let her inside.

"Mom—Mom." Lilah bursts in to a fresh round of applause and tearfully wraps her arms around her mother. "I'm sorry. I'm so, so sorry."

"Shh, shh," Maureen murmurs. "It's okay. It's okay."

"No," Lilah says, hoarsely. "No, it's not okay. Is this art? *This* is fucking art?"

Maureen doesn't have the energy to respond. No, it's not okay, she thinks, wishing she could kick Joe's sleeping head off her bed.

But, yes, she concedes, flinching at the truth of it, yes, all this, all this horror, is art.

She kisses her daughter, smelling the city in her hair, desperate to shed the casts and hold her close.

She tries to block out the next ovation that rises up as a new group pushes in, concentrating instead on maintaining some dignity, and on the sound of Lilah's breath.

OZK

I'll always think of my mother when it snows. When it falls from the clouds wet and heavy, when it drifts down indifferent to gravity on its long, silent journey, when it reaches the earth on a diagonal, each flake tracing the same angle from sky to street, 80°, 80°, 80°; whether it melts upon touching down on rooftops or piles soundlessly on the lawn, when it snows I think of her.

I remember her, years ago, watching it through our living room window. Just standing there, still and staring, short curls framing her ivory cheeks. I took a chance and stood beside her, thinking this might be the time she would put her arm around my shoulders and pull me close to whisper through my hair, "So *beautiful*, isn't it, Margaret?"

She didn't, of course. She didn't move, her arms stayed where they were, hanging by her sides. She couldn't be expected to do the sorts of things that mothers of daughters did, so instead I whispered it for us both as I was then still learning to do: "Beautiful," I said, and looked at her.

Still staring out into the white, the drifting flakes mirrored in her large round glasses, she repeated the syllables of the word. From her lips, though, they were only that. Syllables. Three sounds rubbed clean of connection to each other, to her, to what they were supposed to mean. After a moment she said, with certainty, "Falling thirteen degrees to the perpendicular. With few exceptions. Remarkable if you think of it," then retreated to her study off the kitchen and closed the door.

I pulled a vase off the top of the bookshelf and watched it shatter on the floor. She did not come out. Not a sound from her study. I stomped up the stairs to my bedroom, nearly twisting my ankle as I slapped my stockinged feet against the wood that edged the worn runner, and slammed my door shut. It got stuck in its swollen frame.

Hours later, I heard her downstairs as she swept up the shards with speed and precision.

Once, as a young girl, I was in the back seat of our car drawing pictures with my finger on the steamed-up glass, when she pulled over on the side of the road. She lowered her window and called out, "You're wet! I can drive you."

Through the picture of the sun I'd traced, I saw an old man on an electric scooter, its wheels spinning in the slush. He wore a long grey coat and had a very red nose that stuck out from beneath his snow-piled cap. One of his hands rested limply on his lap while the other gripped the handlebar with fingers white from the cold. I worried that the groceries in the bags tucked under his seat were ruined by the heavy chunks of falling snow and the grey-brown slush that had splattered everywhere.

She didn't give him time to respond. In an instant, she'd yanked up the emergency brake, popped open the trunk and was bent over beside him. She spoke to him briefly before taking his bags and dropping them on the seat beside me, opening and slamming the door in quick succession. The man shrunk into his coat and let the collar ride up over his cheeks. He looked to me like an old and tired turtle. She returned to him with a wool blanket from the trunk and wrapped it around him as he stood up. Together, slowly, they shuffled to the passenger door. The car bounced gently as he let himself fall back into the seat.

She then set to work on the scooter, folding back bars, reducing its proportions by half in seconds before dragging it through the snow to the trunk.

"It took my son three days to figure that out," the man said, watching her through the window. When she disappeared behind the car to heave the scooter in, we turned to look at the snow accumulating on the windshield.

"Your mother is very kind," he said in a rattling voice, setting off a fit of deep mucusy coughs.

Your mother. Is very kind.

"Thank you," I said. With his good hand, he reached into his coat for a handkerchief just as his coughing began to subside.

Your mother is very kind.

She slid back into the car and brushed the snow out of her hair with a quick and deliberate hand.

"Where do you live?" she asked.

I looked at her fogging-up glasses in the rear-view mirror.

Your mother is very kind.

There was a stack of pictures of the two of us in a wintery park. Maybe not quite a stack, maybe there were only a few. One of them in particular stands out in my memory. I'm a baby, four or five months old, bundled in a furry one-piece and lying in her arms. The barren tree branches behind us are lined with white, and beside us is the flat expanse of a frozen pond. She holds me close to her, but something makes her seem uncertain. I remember, as a child, examining my own expression in that photograph to see if even then I could sense her particular distance, but my tiny blurred face was screwed up in the wince made by all babies who are about to cry.

She looks down at me cradled in the nook of her left arm, her right hand bent over my face to protect it from the falling snow. It could almost conjure images of the Virgin and Child.

Almost.

Especially with the luminous white orbs captured in the foreground, it does seem nearly ethereal. But it's the colourlessness, I know, that I loved the most. The pictures could have been in black and white, but they weren't; it was just the winter, the snow that stripped colour away. And for many years I dreamt of doing just that.

———

I was twelve when her pursuit began. One Sunday afternoon that April the door to her study swung open and out she ran right into the kitchen table. A pencil in one hand and papers in the other, she bumped into a door frame, then the banister and then the old rocking chair on her way to where I lay reading in the living room. She sat down on the arm of the couch, out of breath, her lips firing with rapid calculations.

"Mom—what's the matter?" I dropped the book to my lap.

She stared at the wall in front of her, lost in her private language.

"Please, Mom."

"Margaret. I—" Struck by a thought, she scribbled something down.

"Mom!"

She smacked her hand on the papers, squeezed her eyes shut and said, "Margaret, I think I've found another colour," before gathering her notes and walking stiffly back to her study.

—

Dr. Claire Gardner, Associate Professor.
B.Sc. (Toronto), Ph.D. (Yale).
Research fields: mathematical physics, matrix theory,
nonlinear dynamical systems

That was printed beneath her picture in the university's Applied Math Department handbook, the photographer's flash a burst of light in her glasses. I always liked the sound of "matrix theory." I could sense the mystery in the coupling of those words, but I hadn't inherited the aptitude to understand the first thing about the world that carried my mother off for hours and hours every day.

When I was younger I believed she even drifted there in her dreams. Late at night I would creep between the stacks of books in her bedroom to where she lay curled on her bed beside a twisted rope of sheets. I would often have to wrest a notebook from her arms and turn off the lamp on her nightstand or feel around for a pencil beneath her. My eyes would adjust to the moonlight and I'd watch her face to see if I could read what she was dreaming. Her flickering eyelids told me nothing. Sometimes, if her hands weren't tucked between her knees, I'd lift her arm and put it around me and that was how we slept until she turned over to face the other way. When I got cold I'd slip out of her bed and out of her room, and tiptoe back down the hall in darkness.

The morning of that April Sunday, I saw her looking out the living room window as I came downstairs for breakfast. It was dark outside, swells of blowing rain blurring the glass.

"Do you have a good book, Margaret?" she asked when she heard the stairs creak.

A bowl on the kitchen table, a box of Corn Flakes. "Yeah, I think so."

"I have work to do today." She followed me into the kitchen and went to the fridge for milk without reacting to the rip and bang of thunder that tore across the sky.

She always had work to do on Sundays. Most Saturdays too. She'd hole up in her study and tinker with the theory she'd been playing with for years. "Recreation," she called it, as if it was a crossword puzzle, only it didn't fit into a neat square and the solutions didn't arrive with the thud of next week's paper at the front door. Tucked tight between her heavy wooden chair and the expansive desk that had once been my grandparents' dining room table, she sat hunched over for hours, humming, breaking pencil tips with the pressure of her thinking, drinking the cups of black tea and glasses of milk that I alternately took to her at the top of each hour. If there were crumpled-up sheets of paper beneath her I would gather them to toss in the wicker bin, but mostly I sat in the nest of blankets and pillows I'd arranged in the corner of the room, reading or writing stories in my hardbound journal until her humming lulled me to sleep.

I didn't dare bother her with banalities like milk or tea that April day; I knew she wanted to be left alone. And after she'd made her startling pronouncement and went back into her study I barely moved, afraid of disrupting what was unfolding behind her door. Didn't even switch on the lights when the evening began to settle in shadows around me. I wove in and out of sleep, roused periodically by the receding thunder, and finally by her voice, muffled by walls: "Margaret, please order a pizza."

We ate on the living room floor that night amid piles of notes, cups of ginger ale, and tomato sauce-stained paper towels, as she explained how her system of symbols would forever change electromagnetic spectrum theory and prove the existence of another colour. Warped continuums, previously unexplained amplitudes and frequencies, photons, quantum electrodynamics. She said she'd entered a dimension no one had previously considered.

"With my mind, I mean," she said, picking the mushrooms off her slice of pizza. As though I'd think there was a portal hidden by the rug beneath her desk.

I nodded every so often just to keep her going. I had no idea what she was talking about, but there was something in her movements, in her eyes flashing over her notes, in the way she sprung up to get more pop from the fridge, that I never wanted to end. And yet, as I sat chewing on pizza, I sensed a change, a vastness around us. I knew that a tie had been severed and we'd been set adrift, my mother's eyes trained on the horizon, mine on a patch of icy shore slipping further from sight.

Pages and pages filled with notes, supporting proofs, explanations in the margins. More than a decade of work. No one yet could see it.

"It has to be beautiful, Margaret," she said when I found her in her study after school on Monday, still in her pyjamas.

I closed her door and ate leftover pizza for dinner, standing up with my back against the fridge.

She returned to work the next day. And the day after that. And when the summer came she got dressed in the morning and drank her tea before dropping me off at French camp on her way to the university. In the fall, she waved from the screen door when the school bus picked me up at the corner. Unbroken rhythms and routines. The changes were visible only to me in those early days and months. The lengthening of her silences, her gaze a little more faraway than usual. The way she could drift off mid-chew at dinner, a mound of chicken or bread in the pocket of her cheek, and only by banging my glass against the table could I bring her back and set her jaws in motion again. Not that we ate dinner together much by then. Most of the time she'd come home from work, take off her shoes and head straight for her study, and that was where she would stay until long after I'd brushed my teeth and gone to bed.

Two weeks before Christmas I put on my coat and boots, tramped down the hall and announced that I was going to the plaza to buy a tree.

"The tallest one I can find!" I yelled through her door.

I took a step back in the vain hope it might swing open, and then pressed my ear against it, listening for a shuffle of papers or the scrape of her chair against the floor.

Silence.

"I'm getting your wallet!" I called, clomping across the kitchen. "I'm taking fifty dollars!"

Nothing.

I went back to her door and opened it for the first time in months. The lights were off, the blinds drawn.

"Mom?"

A soft voice on the other side of the room. "It's finished."

"Why is it so dark in here?"

"Finished."

I flicked on the switch. She pressed her eyes shut. There were papers everywhere, on the floor, the table. Pencil shavings curled like dead snails. Books open on the ground as if they'd toppled from the shelves. The mouldy smell of old mugs of tea. My mother in her usual place with her arms by her sides, her head bent over a short stack of notebooks as if she hadn't the strength to lift it.

"I'm buying a Christmas tree," I said.

Three blocks from the store, when I knew for certain she hadn't followed me, I turned to go back home. I watched the snow sparkle under the street lights as I kicked it up in puffs. White blinking with tiny shards of colour. Pink, blue, green.

They would think she was a fool.

I'd seen her once before with the other professors and graduate students. A department Christmas party years earlier for the children of faculty. I'd played there with a quiet boy named Winston who'd brought a fire truck and a G.I. Joe that was missing a leg. Santa was a thin pink-faced man in a red plastic costume who bellowed "MERRY CHRISTMAS!" as he leapt into the room and promptly removed his scratchy white beard. Winston was the first kid to get a present and he was told to open it in front of everyone. An abacus. The grown-ups all laughed very hard. Santa then passed him another present, which was a model of the *Millennium Falcon*; *Star Wars* toys for the boys and Strawberry Shortcake dolls for the girls. One girl named Rupinder returned to Santa with a Chewbacca figure, a mistake Santa appeared to feel very bad about.

For the most part, the parents all stayed on one side of the room drinking wine out of paper cups and holding plates of half-eaten potato salad and rolled-up slices of ham. I watched two graduate students approach my mom, who was filling her cup with Coke at the end of the buffet table. She looked at the ground or above their heads as she answered their questions. At one point she scratched the back of her neck and I noticed how inelegant her black digital watch looked resting nearly halfway up her forearm. The other women there, mostly wives with silky hair and sparkly earrings, wore pretty party clothes. Outfits. A blond woman in a tight green turtleneck with a gold chain belt on her hips laughed sweetly at the stories told by the professors around her. I looked at my mother. She was always wearing the same thing: a red plaid shirt, black jeans, brown hiking boots. She checked her watch and said something to the students before retreating to the washroom. The students looked at each other and smirked.

When she came out, she tried to walk unseen past a group of her colleagues, but a man stopped her by the arm and introduced her to some of the wives. She talked to them with her head down, her hands in her pockets. One of the men had a pipe in his teeth; he gently elbowed his wife, who was suppressing a smile. The women examined her with up-and-down eyes while she spoke and closed into a tight circle when she walked away. The man with the pipe let out a hard laugh.

Before she could pour herself more Coke, I told her I was tired and wanted to go home.

"They don't believe me."

She was standing at the door. Chunks of snow that should have been kicked off her boots on the porch were melting into a puddle in the hallway. She looked past me toward the kitchen.

"Gerry said not to submit it. Nonsense, he said it was."

A tide of calm swept over me, reorientation. Relief. The shoreline back in sight.

But then she said, "It's political, I think," and went to her study without taking off her coat or boots.

Castaways once more.

I looked at the slushy grey boot prints she'd left in her wake and wondered what would happen if I let them soak into the floorboards. The old wood had already begun to darken where water bled into the cracks.

In an hour I'd mopped the hallway, the kitchen, the living room and the upstairs. I'd wiped the dust from the banister and the hardened toothpaste from the sink. When I finished in her bedroom I let the mop handle fall from my hands and bang hard against the floor, knowing that she was in her study directly below.

"Don't worry, Mom!" I called. "*I'm okay.*"

I picked up a book from her dresser and smashed the mirror above.

The fragments were still there three days later, crushed to bits where she'd walked over them in her slippers. I swept them into a dustpan and mopped once more to ensure that no pieces were left behind.

A month after I turned eighteen, I left for university. I'd read almost the entirety of my first- and second-year English Lit reading lists by the time I'd arrived, since much of the two years prior I'd spent with my face in a book. Coffee shops, parks. Smoky bars that didn't check ID. My room at night. My mind arcing to the worlds of Woolf, Plath, Brontë, only to retreat to the creaking darkness of our home. My mother had been encouraged to take a sabbatical year, though she never went back to the university when it was over. They'd hoped she'd give up on her theory and spend those months realigning herself. Instead she sank further into it, and further away from me.

I've since heard in hushed confessions from her former colleagues that they never listened when she talked to them about ozk—the name she'd christened her colour, and the term she used as shorthand to describe the math behind it. When she did speak, it was the only thing on her tongue.

"It all just sounded so preposterous," they'd say, and, "Well, you know your mother," with a wink of camaraderie, as though their experience with her was akin to mine.

Now that she can no longer talk, I've often been asked to do so on her behalf. To tell the story of being the daughter of a woman who made such a radical discovery, who gave this gift to the world. To speak about the merit of perseverance in the face of adversity, the value of women in the fields of math and science. "The Mother of Mathematics," the headline had read; strength, serenity and resolve captured in the accompanying photo of her as a graduate student, her chin resting on her hands. God knows where they'd found it.

Her work speaks for itself, I write in my letters back. They say they are impressed by my dignity.

I still wonder if she drifts there in her final human darkness, to her intricate world that begins far beyond the perimeter of my own; or perhaps that is where she now exists entirely. We adjust her bed to a sitting position and she opens her mouth as I feed her spoons of soup or oatmeal. I try to read her eyes but nothing is there.

I direct most inquiries and speaking requests to Jack Springer, the man who brought her work to light. Now a professor himself, he was a graduate student when he unearthed the notebooks my mother had left behind at the university.

"Did she happen to write more?" he'd asked nervously over the phone all those years ago. I told him there were boxes and boxes of notes in her old study. "Would you mind if I came to take a look?"

He's one of the few people I allow to see her as she is now, and the only person to have had intimate access to the workings of her mind. Closer to her, in many ways, than I could ever be. He spoke to her for a long time on his last visit. Leaning forward in the chair with his hands folded and his elbows on his knees, he told her in quiet tones about his trip to Germany and the lab that had harnessed ozk. Wearing special lenses, he'd seen it flash across a screen.

"What does it look like?" I asked later as I walked him to his car.

He smiled. "What does any colour look like? You could have been there if you'd wanted to, Margaret. You know that."

I didn't press. I'd see it soon enough.

"Oh," he said, stopping and reaching into his jacket. "I've been meaning to give you this." He handed me a photograph of my much-younger mother standing in a winter park with a baby in her arms. "I found it before my trip. It was tucked in a file with some old notes. I thought I'd given it to you years ago."

I stared at the picture, the way her hand shielded my face from the falling snow.

"I haven't seen this in ages. I wonder why it was in there."

Jack looked at me strangely. "Turn it over."

On the back, in her hand, the word *OZK* was written beside the year I was born. And beneath it: *the sound Margaret made when snow first touched her face.*

BARBADOS

Each morning, I watch from our open window as the woman and the man drag their loungers out along the soft pale sand to reserve the same spots under the same palm trees by the same violent, indifferent waves, wordlessly draping the white weathered vinyl with blue beach towels and tossing down straw hats and paperback novels and bottles of sunscreen before retreating back up the stone steps toward the villas and, presumably, back to bed. I turn from the shutters, your body still a sleeping lump on your side of the ginormous bed, close to the edge.

Hours later, the bronzed sixty-something platinum-haired wife comes out in her white bikini to reclaim her chair. Her eyes fixed on the ruler line that keeps the sea from the sky, all above and below it blue and foamy white. She doesn't acknowledge us. But why should she when we are just renting? We're only here for the week, and when we drive our rental car back to the airport our faces will dissolve from her memory, as will our naive self-conscious appreciation of the rollicking sea and the gentle shifts in the breeze and the warm sand under our feet. Tiring to witness, week after week, we (our kind) must be to her. She rubs oil into her thin brown biceps as if she can't see us tripping past with our cumbersome umbrella and our bag of toys and our SPF-55 and our three fraying towels and this baby in a sun-protective suit, hooded, on my hip. You dig a hole deep enough in which to jam the umbrella pole and I make a point of thinking that I won't remember her face either. It's dissolving already, as soon as I look away. You get the pole in, packing the sand around it to make it sturdy, and I put the baby down on a towel in its shadow.

"Germans," you say as if it's an explanation, jutting your chin at the woman and clapping sand from your hands. I laugh, maybe too eagerly, lapping up this first taste of levity in weeks.

"Totally," I say, just to say something, but you're already walking away. I watch you disappear up the steps and around the corner. I shouldn't have laughed, shouldn't have said anything at all. Or maybe I should have said more. And now it's not clear if you're coming back.

I throw the blankets to the floor. The clash of midnight waves resounding through the open window. Lit with terror, I feel around desperately in the sweaty sheets.

"Where is she?" I push you aside, bracing myself to find her there, flattened and blue in the moonlight.

"Natalie! Calm down. Calm. *Down*." You pin my arms

to my sides, your hold more like a straitjacket than an embrace. "Breathe."

The panic still fizzes on my skin long after I realize she's in her crib, asleep.

The German woman squints at her novel, periodically rubbing her pedicured big toes together. I dig a hole in the sand and fill it with water for the baby to splash, noting, from the corner of my eye, how the German's cellulite doesn't look so bad because it's tanned through. I wonder how many months it would take to get a tan like that, how many day after day after days of exactly this it would take. She lays her book down beside her and closes her eyes and lets her feet flop out to the sides.

Corpse pose, I think. The very attainment, the very attainment of peace.

I dig another hole, and another, and fill them with water that just gets absorbed. The baby cries out so I fill them all again.

We let the seafoam lick the baby's toes. She is still learning to walk and has never felt sand beneath her feet until now. It was a long winter. She holds our fingers as we run up and down the edge of the sea.

"The ocean kissed your toes! The ocean kissed your toes!" we cry out, acting joyful. She stops to watch, to feel it wash over and recede. Her chubby little feet. One time a wave comes further in than we expect and she gets splashed in the face. The salt, the wet shock of it. The betrayal. The knowledge now that even if we're right here, even if we're holding on, something bad can happen. This makes me feel worse than the water and salt in her eyes, and that is why I scooped her up and held her like that, against your protests. The German husband is out now and both of them are on their loungers squinting at their books, unspeaking, acting like they can't hear us. I'm mad as I wrap her up in the towel and pull her against my chest, marching back to the villa as you yell at me over the clamour of the sea. You say I'm over-reacting and that she might as well learn that shit happens. I don't want to respond but that pierces right deep into the mess of it all and I stop and glare at you over my shoulder because, really, *really*, what the fuck is that supposed to mean? Our eyes meet for a flash before I take off again for the rented apartment we're supposed to call a villa, and I see you see that you hurt me. I look for regret in your expression, and maybe there's a shard of it there somewhere but it's impossible to tell if it's about what you just said or everything else. I press her against me and accidentally kick up a lot of sand as I tread by the Germans, noticing as I pass that their loungers aren't even close, aren't even parallel to each other.

The very attainment of peace.

Everyone said:

Make sure you go away on your mat leave! Go when she's still a baby. She flies for free! And, oh my gosh, she's so transportable. Just wait, just wait until she's a toddler! Haha. Just wait until you have two! Hahaha. Then you're screwed. Haha. And anyway, you've got all this time now, a whole year!

What they didn't say is that she'll scream and cry and shake the bars of her rickety rented crib for hours every night until she goes hoarse and collapses with defeated exhaustion because no, this isn't her bed, and no, this isn't her room, and no, this isn't the way the light is supposed to be or the heat or the sounds or the smells or anything, any part of this.

Get me the fuck out of here! it sounds like she's screaming as we lie in the dark on our gigantic bed, watching the uneven bamboo fan wobble and click round and round and I agree, I completely agree, and when I start to cry too you get up and punch the sheets on your side over and over with both fists, your face contorted, your bare feet slapping against the tiles as you stomp off to the balcony.

"I can't deal with this," you shout over her screams. "I'm not dealing with this shit."

I make myself believe you're just talking about the baby because otherwise

Otherwise what?

Otherwise would be impossible. Otherwise would be unbearable.

The din of the ocean roars through the open balcony door and mutes again when you slam it shut. I lift the sobbing, arching child and say *Shhh, shhh*, and bop around, dancing, pretending to be in control, until her head is heavy on my shoulder and all of us are quiet again.

———

In the morning, you come out onto the balcony where the baby is splashing in a roasting pan and I'm watching the waves roll in toward the Germans dozing on their loungers below. You drag over a chair and take my feet from where they rest on the ledge and lay them on your lap. I don't know how to react. I don't move.

"Paradise," you say after a minute.

I nod. "Yes, it really is."

"Can you imagine waking up here for months?" You peer over the ledge at the Germans.

"No, I can't." I am crushed by my desire to be these people we're being right now.

"Paradise," you say, more thoughtfully this time, putting my feet back on the ledge.

You lean over to kiss the baby's blond curls on your way back inside to get coffee or take a shit, and I can hear Bob Marley on the stereo as you open the door. I'd put on the same album when we packed for this trip, "Three Little Birds" playing as we silently folded T-shirts and bathing suits, stuffed our toiletry bags with razors and toothpaste and sunblock. I'd finally sat down on the edge of our bed and said, "Why are we doing this? Forget it. This is crazy. Let's just cancel."

"And what? Throw four grand down the drain? No thanks."

You still couldn't look at me then. You went back into the bathroom to get your shaving cream.

I see you hunched over your phone through the balcony door, checking your email or looking something up. You fade into the dark of the hallway, your head down.

"Nat?" you call from the bed. "Natalie?"

You're trying to be quiet so the baby doesn't wake up.

"What are you doing?" you whisper-call.

I've been sitting on the toilet too long. Everything about me feels different. My skin, my hands, the smell of my pee. I want you to get out of bed, to come in, to squat down in front of me and say *Hey, hey, come here, come here* and hold my teary wet face and then hug me as I finally let go and cry into your bare sunburnt shoulder. I'll tell you how scared I am and you can then say, *Shhh, shhh, it's okay, it's really going to be okay.*

"Natalie?"

"Yeah."

"You okay?"

"Yeah."

"Don't fall asleep in there or anything."

By four on a Wednesday I still hadn't heard. I called the doctor's office.

Please hold, all our agents are currently helping other callers.

Please note, test results won't be given over the phone. Please book an appointment with your doctor to discuss test results.

A receptionist picks up. I tell him I'm waiting for test results.

He looks up my file. I can hear him typing. He's quiet for a few long seconds, the rhythm of his breath changing. I try not to read into it. He says my doctor isn't in today, but the supervising doctor will call me back.

The baby naps for an hour in the morning, and when you find me hovering over her crib, stroking her head, you say, "Enough. Just go down to the beach or something."

"Okay, maybe."

"Give me your phone."

"But—"

"If it rings, I'll call you. Just go."

I don't waste time pulling out a lounger. I carry my bag and beach towel past the German wife, who's lying prostrate with her eyes closed. I'm aware of her disapproval even though she can't see me. Lying on a towel right on the sand is for locals. Not for villa tenants. I flap out my towel, trying to get it to lie flat despite the wind off the ocean. It keeps getting blown in a wrinkled sandy heap. I smooth it out with my hands. The wife rolls over. I take out the *Hello!* magazine I brought from upstairs, my iPod, earbuds, put them all beside me, then I just sit there, looking out at the clear sky, the waves, the way they disrupt the pebbles. A vicious tsunami every few seconds, from the pebbles' perspective. After a while, a tiny crab emerges from a hole in the sand and skitters sideways away from us.

———

"The baby is fine," the supervising doctor said. "Her blood work is completely normal."

"Oh my God, thank Christ." The tears bursting through a dam. "And thank you, I mean, I know you're not supposed to give results on the phone—"

"We're going to need you to get tested again. We think your sample may have been compromised in the lab. We've sent in a requisition already." Papers rustled in the new quiet between us. "They're calling it inconclusive."

A ringing in my ears, an unwavering high-pitched tone. My saliva dried up.

"But what . . . what does that mean—*inconclusive*? It's negative, right? I mean, my husband is negative. The baby now, like you just said . . ." I let that evidence hang out there, to convince him.

The doctor paused. He seemed to be reading something. "There was an error in the lab," he said. "They've asked us to send you back in. I'm sure it's nothing to be overly worried about."

The baby started to cry upstairs, her nap over. I glanced over at the time on the microwave. Twenty minutes early. I felt like my lungs were shrinking.

"I'll have Dr. Myers call you when she's in tomorrow. I'll tell her you're coming in. Some time over the next couple of days?" He was beginning to sound rushed. "And you'll be able to move forward from there. Sound good?"

"We're leaving for Barbados," I said. "We leave on Saturday."

"Well, the lab's open tomorrow. Or you can just leave it until you get back. I mean, at this stage . . ." Rustling papers again.

"At this stage . . . ?"

He cleared his throat. "You're in a committed relationship?"

"I'm married."

"And your husband's been tested?"

"Negative." I started to shake. "I mean, he's negative."

"Well, that's a good thing. Isn't it?"

I walk out into the water. I wish I'd brought one of the inflatable rafts from the storage cage that belongs to our unit. I'd like to ride the waves. The surfers are coming out now. I watch the youngest ones with their sun-bleached hair and their wiry brown bodies paddle out beyond the rocky outcropping. I kneel down on the shallow ocean floor and let a wave crash into me. It's warm. I'm all wet now, my hair in my face. I let another crash over, and the next, and the next. My body tenses, as if I'm holding on to something. Like if all my muscles are clenched, I can't get taken down by the undertow that's tugging hard at my legs. I stand tall again but the next step takes me deeper than I expect. I lose my footing and the undertow is a whole other ocean beneath the one I entered so thoughtlessly a minute ago, its powerful and unpredictable current swayed by some mad underworld moon. Another wave crashes over me. I didn't see this one coming and it knocks the air from my lungs. Salt water stings my eyes, my nostrils, the taste of it in my throat. I lose sense of when and where to gasp for air, the tenseness in my body futile, holding on to nothing but itself.

We were watching *Downton Abbey* when I got the call. My legs were on your lap. The youngest daughter was campaigning with the suffragette movement and falling in love with the wrong kind of man. The Irish driver. My phone rang and the number was unaccompanied by a photo or a name, but for some reason I picked it up anyway.

"Hello?"

"Natalie."

I knew who it was right away, even though it had been years. His voice gravelly, unmistakable, urgent.

"Hey," I said, trying to sound like it was one of my friends, hoping the rush of colour to my cheeks was unseeable in the TV light. Like it was just Vanessa or Jill or Camille. Not the Drummer. Not the guy I'd fucked in the bathroom of a Parkdale bar (and the balcony of his apartment, and the studio where he rehearsed) when I'd only been married six months. Not the reason for the airless black crater into which we'd tumbled and out of which we'd barely been able to scratch our way.

"Hey, what's going on?" I said, kicking my legs off your lap, trying to infuse my voice with both a breeziness for your benefit and a bored malevolence for his. I picked up my water glass and casually headed for the kitchen.

"Want me to pause it?" you said, holding up the remote.

No, I mouthed. Gesturing I'd be right back.

"Natalie," the Drummer said.

The Drummer whose nose you dislocated with your novice yet impressive right hook when we ran into him outside a different Parkdale bar, who was out having a smoke on the sidewalk between sets, his drumsticks in the back pocket of his ripped jeans as he chatted up some wide-eyed smirking brunette a year after I'd followed him down the narrow stairs of the dive three doors down, the brick walls on either side painted night with constellations.

I'm sorry, I'm sorry, I'm sorry, I'd cried to you, literally on my knees, when I couldn't not tell you any longer because I realized I wanted to be with you after all, despite the unexamined years that had led to an unexamined marriage and its unexamined quiet hostility and I said it was because of my father being sick and the stress of everything but still now I don't know why really, why I let it all go and just said fuck it. You, how you stood there silent, unknowable, with your forehead resting on the fridge. You left for two days and when you came back I didn't ask why or where, and couldn't even handle the possibility of a who—all that mattered was that you came back. Oh, the soaring relief of it all when we stood at the door, crying into each other for radically different reasons. I felt like someone had lifted a lead X-ray blanket off my body.

My hand quivered as I turned on the tap. "Why are you calling me?"

The Drummer took a deep breath. "I'm calling because I have a responsibility to tell you something." The words sounded official, practised.

I truly thought right then that he was doing the 12 steps. That he was calling to make amends. I truly thought that I would hear him out and forgive him for almost fucking up my marriage or whatever it was that he thought he had done and then you and I would go back to watching *Downton Abbey*.

Strange things happen when you're drowning. Body parts flail on their own accord, your lungs, heart, brain going into some kind of survival overdrive. Fight or flight. The sea already had me in its grips so I couldn't flee, but I could fight, hence the flailing, the punching at water. But in the midst of the panic there's a quiet rippling so deep below the bedrock of consciousness it's less thought than wordless possibility and from there rises the idea: Why not just let go?

After we survived what we thought was the worst thing—the infidelity, the invasion of another body into our sacred union, etc. etc. etc.—we swore to complete transparency, believing it was the only way we'd make it. And until that moment, we'd more or less followed through. No secrets. Sunday night tête-à-têtes wherein everything was on the table. Minor crushes that pulsed at work, irritants between us that threatened to ignite if left untended. Uncertainties. But when you found me crumpled on the kitchen floor, my face in my hands, my phone thrown to the other side of the room, I had no answer for you as you asked over and over, What? What is it? Who was that? Natalie, please, sweetheart, what's going on?

Because, tell me, what are the words for that? There wasn't a verb, an adjective, a person place or thing that could convey the horror, the loneliness over which I was perched, the vacuum of it. The absence of even an echo.

"Natalie—what?" You held my shoulders. "What about her?"

Only then did I hear myself repeating the baby's name.

In the churning, the flailing, the fight, I thought of her in the way that thoughts can span years in an instant. I thought of her grown up, in her twenties, standing before grey crashing waves, hurling tearful unhearable insults at a pitiless sea. Would that be better? I wondered, gasping, gulping lungfuls of salt water. Better than growing up with a marked mother whose hand no one would shake? Who's whispered about in grocery aisles as she pushes her child in the cart, perusing the cereals, each step closer to the grave? A veil of tragic beauty draped over the child's head, the motherless-child-to-be, oblivious, kicking her legs, pleading for Frosted Flakes. The child who could instead become the drunk and high twenty-something dancing in spinning circles on some godforsaken beach, tears in her eyes as she looks up searching for her mother in the stars. A lover, craving her from the periphery, waits without interfering because he heard somewhere that her mother drowned long ago. The beauty and her mother, a star. A fucking star. And she would be so beautiful, wouldn't she? With that sadness always just there on her skin, that absence so present. *Motherless.* Me, the mother, a dreamy kitchen dancer, barely preserved in warped flashes of memory. Isn't that how it goes? Or not even that, not even that, because what do we remember from before we were one year old? And you,

you.

Her sad beauty crushing you as you watch her grow, as you slip through the years together to the day she's on a beach and you're in your living room staring at her picture, praying she is all right. It is so hard not to reach out to hold her always. To touch her, like your replacement wife will do to you often, your wobbly resilience so in need of tender care.

No. It will not be like that at all. You will shed your dead love for me and emerge with wings you didn't know you had and your replacement wife will marvel at your metamorphosis. She will be a strong one, someone whose anchors will not give way, but she'll have kind, wet eyes as she squeezes your shoulder, and you will not have to say anything to each other at all because there will be no secrets and she will just understand. She'll keep her hand on you because you've already been through so much, and no matter what next, her anchors will not give way.

Is it time to panic?

Up down flipped around. Defenceless against the lunacy of the sea, its merciless current. I see a flash of someone, a man standing on the rocky outcrop, watching me. Is it you? Please. Please let it be you. Please be the one to save me.

It's not you. He's blond. Tanned. Looking for me to give him a sign. A signal maybe, to show I'm not just playing around. I can't catch my breath. I don't know when the sky will be there and I can breathe it in. Maybe it's better it's not you. Maybe you've saved me too many times and this time you would just watch me go under. Nothing is predictable.

I gasp when the sky appears and he's crouched down in an athletic pose, yelling something. *You stupid girl who got herself in this mess*, maybe, *you helpless idiot who's going to get herself killed*.

Sharp, jagged pain.

My left ankle twists, my right foot feels like it's being dragged over a cheese grater. But oh my God, sweet mercy: at least, at the very least this is land, sweet fucking land.

The blond man yanks me up by my armpits, pulls me out of the murderous sea and drops me onto the sand.

"Shit," he says, bending over with his hands on his knees, catching his breath. "Shit." The waves pulled my bikini bottoms halfway down my legs, my top untied, covering nothing.

"You okay?" He yells it at my face the way my mother yells into the phone when it's long distance. "Hey!" He slaps my cheek. "Can you hear me?"

I want to sleep.

"Hey—Steve!" the hero cries down the beach. "Call for help!"

I can tell by the way he says *shit* again, he's looking at my feet.

There is shouting in the distance. It is your voice, coming toward us.

"Wait!" I hear you call, running. "Don't touch her!"

It sounds like the territorial cry of a jealous husband but I know it's not me or you or us you're protecting, but my rescuer who is about to touch my bloodied foot.

"I want to be able to hold you. I want so badly to hold you now and tell you we'll get through this," you said, looking out the dark kitchen window, crying. "But I can't."

I could not stand up. I'd vomited and it was all over my hands. I saw the back of your head and the lines the comb had made in your hair that morning.

"I swear to God, Natalie. I swear to God. If there's something wrong with her—"

You choked. Your knees buckled. I reached out for you but there was too much space between us.

"Please," I said, still reaching. "Please. I can't breathe."

When you couldn't stand any longer you slumped down beside me. You put your arms around me. It was a desperate act. It was a Hail Mary to find something to hold on to, to find out if it was worth holding on at all.

And then, when nothing was better, when I felt how far away you were, you let go.

The German wife is holding my cheek against her bare warm belly, my head on her lap. Her hair now an aureole of white around the shadow of her face, her head blotting out the sun. Her voice is lower than I expected, more nuanced, as she directs the blond hero to get certain things: antiseptic, wide bandages, latex gloves. "It will suffice till we get her to hospital," she's saying. And she's British, not German. She looks down at me.

"Natalie?" She sounds like Emma Thompson, warm, in control. "Natalie? Can you hear me. I'm Dr. Paula Stevens. You're in shock."

You are holding the baby a few feet away. Swaying together, watching me.

"Natalie—you've broken your ankle. We'll brace it here, get it set at hospital. Good as new before you know it."

The wind picks up and blows a lot of sand around. You hold up a hand reflexively to protect the baby's face. She lunges toward me, kicking her feet and whelping, arms stretched out. I reach back for her, but I am lying on the sand. I cannot hold her here, and I cannot hold her the way I want to, I cannot need her like this. She's a child, not a life raft. I keep reaching, however weakly, but now my eyes are on you and you do not move.

The blond hero trots back with an armload of supplies. The doctor takes the gloves first and puts them on. She lowers my head onto a towel that's been folded to make a firm pillow and sets to work on my ankle. I am watching the blues and greens and whites of the waves and sky and palms, missing the closeness, the warmth of her body.

Hold on to me.

"What?" she says.

I close my eyes. Pain shoots up my leg.

———

You're sitting on a cracked vinyl chair with the baby on your lap. I'm in a hospital bed beside you. My leg is in a cast, raised by straps hooked to the ceiling. Air conditioning rumbles; a ceiling fan click click clicks.

"Give her to me." I push myself up. I am groggy, floating.

You hand me my phone instead. There's a missed call from my doctor back home. Everything is moving.

"Give her to me," I repeat, putting the phone down on the bed.

"Call," you say. "Call now."

The baby squeals and smiles at me. She stretches out her arms and kicks her legs as though she's trying to swim through the air. You relent and let her lead you up out of the chair toward me. You put her in my arms and stand there beside us, protectively, and we seem just as we were in the seconds after she was born.

I pick up my phone and call the doctor and you move to take the baby from me as the line rings and the recording tells me to hold. I turn from you and hold her tighter and the recording says they do not give results over the phone. She is snug against my chest. She is smiling and looking across the room at the window. I crumble a little when you put your hand on my shoulder but I do not cry. The receptionist answers and I say who I am and where I am and that I am returning Dr. Myers' call. My voice echoes in my head and in my chest and across the ocean. I let your hand stay where it is, I let myself believe you won't let go if I get taken under.

The doctor says she'll cut right to it and I am holding the baby and rocking and the crying isn't crying but a tsunami howling to the surface from beneath something that cracked apart inside me long ago. And she is saying, I know, I know, you must be very relieved, as I'm almost choking on all the wet flowing from my eyes and nose and mouth. I rock the baby and hold her against me and your hand slips away as you walk to the window, wiping your eyes. Your back to us as the doctor says, So Barbados, huh? It really is paradise, isn't it? And when I can't answer she says, softly, Well, now you can enjoy it.

I hang up and you are a silhouette at the window, looking out over some place I can't see. We must be far from the water because for the first time since we got here I hear no waves. Just the clicking ceiling fan, the rumbling AC, the rattle of my own breath as I struggle to catch it. The baby babbles in my arms, her small hand wrapped around my index finger. I kiss her head and pull her as close as I can, but, of course, that won't be enough. It could never be enough.

It has to be enough, for now.

DISTANCE

3.7

Miles or kilometres? Nothing on the display to indi-cate either. Just 3.7. Almost 3.8 now, which Mark knows because of the green dots that make their way around the digital track, slowly tracing a full oval before disappearing altogether and starting again from nothing.

For a second he thinks that kilometres are longer than miles, but knows that is only because the word itself stretches further along a page. Miles are longer. These are miles. They feel like miles. Twenty-six and change in a marathon. Not that he's ever run that many at once.

Sweat stings his eyes and he has to wipe them with his T-shirt. He forgot his towel in the locker room. If he had a towel he would throw it over the display so he wouldn't look at it so much.

Still 3.8.

The gym is in Canada so the display should be in kilo-metres, but he thinks that the treadmill was probably made in the U.S. or, at least, for American consumers and nobody cares enough to convert the readings to metric. That's just the way things are. He thinks there should be a law like the one ensuring that milk is sold in litres and meat in grams, and a government rep with a clipboard who comes around to check that all the displays are in kilometres. Or maybe that isn't a law, maybe it's just an agreement between the manufacturers and grocery stores. All he knows is that he doesn't buy a quart of milk, he buys a litre. Just one now. For his coffee, and for his cereal when he has some in the cupboard, which is rarely. Any more than a litre and it goes bad.

A soapy mop slaps against the outside of the window beside him, catching him off guard. He almost falls off the treadmill but regains his footing just in time. The mop is worked up and down by a thin man, shirtless and tanned to leather, like he hasn't been inside since the start of summer. Even now, the evening sun looms over his shoulder as if baking him dry. He wears tattered jean shorts, a straw hat and a dingy hemp necklace that looks like it smells sour, like old urine. A cigarette dangles between his withered lips while he reaches high to the top of the window with his mop, squinting against the rising smoke.

No one walking past pays any attention to the window cleaner. The sky behind him is a hazy vermillion. The sun is sinking fast. It's a perfect red-orange circle and you can stare right at it while it goes down behind the city, behind the man. Mark would like to tell someone to turn and see it before it disappears. See, it's almost gone already. Along the row of treadmills everyone is looking forward, though, mostly at the TV screens attached to their machines, little white buds in their ears. Mark turns back to look. The window cleaner winks.

—

Out over the weathered deck, through the tall, sparse, blowing grass, Mark saw her sitting on the sand. The lake and sky were the same blank grey, the horizon nearly indiscernible where their expanses smeared into one beyond her.

Ice bobbed in his drink. He threw it back.

Elise wore his old brown wool sweater, usurped for campfires and late-night conversations with neighbours on the deck, holes now where her thumbs poked through. He hadn't been ready to surrender it to the sand and smoke of cottage life, the sweater he'd worn each Saturday morning for years as a matter of routine perhaps more than preference, but the moment she slipped it on he knew it was lost to her.

The wind loosened a lock of hair from her ponytail. She tucked it behind her ear, the too-long sweater sleeve covering her palm.

He turned up the stereo and went back to the kitchen to pour another drink. He drank it down, too fast, as if to numb something, as if there was some pain to quiet. But there wasn't. So maybe it was the opposite. He poured a third to instead awaken a whole part of him that had shut down, to shock it the fuck to life.

He opened his throat like a chute. Electric paddles to the ribs.

Clear.

He poured another.

Clear.

He added a handful of ice to the next, and felt a tiny flicker, a feeble pulse, as he looked out at her on his way back to his leather recliner. The briefest plummet of sadness. Hard to tell for who, though, or about what.

He sunk back into his chair, feet up, and cranked the volume loud to feel his muscles, his organs, his eardrums, his heart twitching to the beat of some, of any, rhythm.

The lake was choppy and churning, swirling grey into black, low white peaks crashing down and stretching out over the dark wet sand spotted with shells. For a Southern Ontario lake it could perform an excellent impression of the Atlantic. Elise tried to block out the woods lining the periphery, tried to envision a rocky coast beneath her, but she could only be where she was. Sand stuck to her legs, the cottage behind her, their words and anger still echoing in the trees. Blame and contempt and you, you, you, how you've failed me, crescendoing in a closed-fist wallop that had stunned them both silent. The ringing in her ears hadn't stopped. At least now the mending was up to him. At least now she got to be the sullen, quiet, outraged one passing from room to room with a clenched jaw or looking out over the lake, waiting for him to break, to beg, to return to the same knee on which he'd asked for her hand, exchanging that happy sentiment for teary contrition as he pled for her mercy. She listened to the waves, pricking up her ears each time she thought she heard the deck door slide open or the crunch and rustle of his runners in the grasses.

A pack of cigarettes that she didn't really want lay at her feet with a lighter perched on top. She hadn't smoked in months but had grabbed them from the cupboard on top of the fridge on her way out the door as if she'd never quit. Mark kept extras in case a guest wanted one, a supposed habit of hospitality bequeathed by his parents, but she knew they were really for those frequent nights when he was left alone with Neil Young and the dying fire.

The rhythm of the waves finally began to lull her elsewhere, nowhere, an empty place of some reprieve, until the whir and chop of a Jet Ski crossing the wake of a power boat brought her back again. She wondered how much had been heard around the lake—voices carried well—and imagined, as she lit a cigarette, a young couple cuddling by a bonfire with a bottle of red wine, cringing as the argument rippled over the calm water, so pleased with themselves for choosing a partner with whom that would never, ever happen, knowing with such desperate certainty that it could never, ever be them.

Elise wanted to be snapping the ends off of asparagus in the kitchen, sipping on pinot gris. She wanted to go back to that, to the hope of a peaceful dinner, to a quiet night curled in front of a movie while he nodded off in his chair. She listened again for Mark's approach but heard only the buzz of the Jet Ski getting further away.

——

Mark winced at the sound of her voice. The false cheer of it. The fact that she'd answered.

"Oh," he said. "I didn't think I'd catch you. I thought you had a meeting."

"It was cancelled. I was just picking up some pasta for dinner."

"Yeah, I was going to leave a message. I think I'm going to head up north tonight."

She paused. "Okay."

"So don't get anything for me."

She didn't respond. He rolled his eyes and tapped the steering wheel with his index finger, his blood pressure rising as her silence pressed against him. He flicked on the indicator to merge onto the two-lane cottage highway.

"Hello?" he said after a minute. "So, we good?"

"It's just . . ."

"What?"

She took a deep breath. "Maybe it wouldn't be the worst thing, if you came home."

Home. Elise quiet, bent over the counter, her face stony as she chopped vegetables he wouldn't eat. Home. Elise clacking down the plates and telling him some anodyne tidbit about something she'd read on Twitter, about what someone had said at work, cutting the tension with the dullest blade. Home. Her expectation from across the table's divide, that he'd grunt, nod, say something equally unprovocative in response. Waltzing through a minefield, word by word, gesture by gesture, until it was just late enough for her to go to bed.

"I want to take care of the leaves."

"Maybe I'll come up, then."

"I don't think so."

"Why?"

"Come on, Elise. Just, come on."

A warning in her inhalation. His irritation danger-ously asymptotic to the black hole. The liquor store was up ahead, the last one before the turnoff. He checked the time on the dash. He could just make it.

"I'll see you tomorrow?" he said into the nothing of the car.

Silence. He pulled into the lot, saw a clerk look out the glass door. Mark waved. Held up a finger, made the sign of being on the phone.

"I'm going to go, Elise. I'm going to hang up now."

"Wait—"

"I gotta go. Client calling on the other line. I'll talk to you later, okay?"

Nothing.

"Okay?"

"Yeah, okay. I just—"

Mark disconnected the call. He jumped out of the car and jogged to the store entrance. He hadn't hung up on her. She'd said okay. It was easy to pretend he hadn't heard the rest. He was already thinking of the fire he'd build. The grip on his chest loosening. The place all to himself. He would get the best red they had here. Two. He would get a good enough Scotch. He smiled at the clerk as he clanked the bottles on the counter. So much easier to breathe. He made a joke. They laughed together, like everything was great. It was going to be a good night.

On a city morning Elise woke to him beside her, asleep and heavy. An entire universe in a breathing mass. Sunlight filtered twice—once through the shifting leaves of the tree outside the window, then through the cracks in the blinds—animated the curves of his body.

Elise, he'd whispered in the dark as he got into bed the night before, mouthwash failing to camouflage the smoke and whisky on his breath.

Elise, hey—his voice gay with the artificial lift of what he'd drunk. He'd pressed closer, naked, thrusting a lump at her back.

Eyes wide, Elise had stared at the opposite wall, moderating her breath to mimic sleep. She didn't move as he'd fumbled with his weak erection between her thighs.

Elise, come on.

His hand suddenly up and into her. She'd kicked his leg as though she was dreaming.

Fuck this, he'd said, withdrawing and flipping over, pulling the blanket off her.

She'd stared at the wall, stung, silent, waiting for him to storm out with his pillow. But his breathing deepened, and the snores rolled in. Rhythmic enough, at least, after a while, to pull her under, too.

In the morning she slipped out from beneath the covers without sound, without catching the sheets, and took five long steps to the door, avoiding the creaks under the rug.

She turned to look at him. His stillness roused an old sadness in her, a passing desire to retreat, to fit her body into his, to press her nose to his neck and inhale. But the impulse wasn't strong and she was in the hall with the door shut behind her before he could sense that she'd gone. She had perfected her escape.

She didn't know that he shifted his bulk to turn to the ghost she'd left behind, to put his hand in her absence carved into the sheets, warm and wrinkled in the place where she'd lain.

He didn't know that she stood on the other side of the door in the hallway so she could feel the cold air on her skin. Hairs stand up, goosebumps rise, nipples stiffen. She breathed in slow and deep before getting her robe from the bathroom, shivering as she wrapped it around her on her way to the kitchen to start her day.

Mark liked his condo. Liked the way the key slid into the lock without having to be jiggled around. Liked the dim mirrored elevator that didn't take too long, the quiet dishwasher, the firm grey couch and chairs that had come with the place. Liked stacking his black-spined magazines chronologically on his bookshelf, liked wiping the clean white block of a peninsula that separated the kitchen from the living room, liked sweeping the small triangular balcony with its view of the lake. You could only see it on clear days, and by looking through the gap between two other buildings, but still it was there. A lake view. Friends remarked on it before saying, "Nice pad, man. Awesome place for a transition."

And when he reminded them that it'd been nearly two years, they'd just smile and grip his shoulder and say, "Give it time, bro, give it time," mistaking his hollowness for something buried and heading to the fridge for a beer.

He wouldn't tell the women he met about the lake view. The reality would never compare. Instead, he'd keep the blinds open when he expected to bring someone home and let her discover it herself while he casually opened a bottle of wine on the peninsula.

"Oh my gosh. Mark? Is that the lake over there?"

"Oh, yeah. It's a little hard to see right now."

"Wow, what a beautiful view," she'd say while accepting her glass of wine and squinting into the dark.

Elise opened the cupboard and a bag of cookies fell out. The bag wasn't sealed properly and before it even hit the ground, a cookie smashed against the countertop and crumbled to bits on the floor. She tried not to cry as she picked up the crumbs with a damp paper towel and wondered what would happen. She ground the beans and thought about how she could wait until he'd left the house, how she could drive away.

"Elise?" he called from behind the bathroom door. "Are there any clean towels?"

"Yes," she yelled back, such relief in the sound of her own voice, the way it just carried on. "In the closet. I did a load yester—"

The hiss of the shower. He couldn't hear her anymore.

She dumped four tablespoons into the filter and poured four cups of water into the back.

She decided to try something. With the shower running, with the coffee maker choking and burping, she turned toward the bathroom and said out loud, "I don't love you anymore," just to see what it felt like, before taking two mugs from the cupboard and a single spoon from the drawer. She tore a jagged triangle off the roll of paper towels to wipe her cheeks and nose, then clicked on the news to check the weather.

None of the women lasted more than a few dates, all of them pretty and just young enough to not be pricked by his indifference, to not sour at his state of impermanence. Only one ever mentioned the fire, and even then, it was only after they'd smoked a joint and got into the cognac following several bottles of wine.

"I remember your picture in the paper," she'd said with a dull smile and smeared eyeliner, their clothes scattered around the living room. "I didn't want to say before, but I remembered. Seems like forever ago now, kinda."

"Yeah, I guess. I try not to think about it much."

"What happened again? A barbecue or something?"

"Propane tank." He sat up and lit the roach that was lying in the ashtray. Inhaled. "Faulty line. Whole cottage went up."

"Right. *Right*. Shit." She shook her head and took the roach from him with experienced pincer fingers. "Shit, eh?" she said, inhaling, a look of hazy contemplation passing over her face. She exhaled and passed it back. "Shit."

"Don't worry about it. Happened a long time ago." He took a pull off what remained.

"Yeah. But still."

When he was out with a widow, which happened once, she'd asked how his wife passed away; an absence she felt at liberty to probe, and did so with the compassionate tone of shared experience. But a fire wasn't the same as cancer or a stroke, and he'd watched her eyes as he morphed into a character in some greater and more exquisite tragedy.

The how-you-holding-ups, long looks and arm squeezes dissipated with time, as did the phone calls from her sisters. And outside of the yearly invitation to a Christmas party thrown by her old roommate, Mark stopped hearing from her friends as well. As for the few people left in his life who had known them both, no one asked why there weren't any pictures of her anywhere in his condo, why nothing remained to show she'd existed in his world at all. They all assumed that her wedding ring was tucked in a velvet box near the front of his sock drawer, or carefully placed in a hidden shrine they imagined he'd visit in his lowest hours, where he'd finger the cork of the champagne bottle popped on their engagement and look at photos of her kissing a statue in the lobby of a Paris hotel. They'd been so in love, after all.

No one imagined the nowhere into which he'd been flung, a grief-less place with no edges. Even when he burned everything that remained, still, there were no edges.

—

5.9

He'll make it to six and that's enough. That must be almost ten kilometres, though he isn't sure of the exact conversion. The ache in his knees and the fire in his lungs won't let him continue much longer. It's not that he has anywhere to be. Everyone else on the row of treadmills is in between the pull of one place and another. Work and home, he guesses, or for the tougher guys, the reverse. He looks in the mirror at the bouncing faces lit by the glow of their televisions—faces suppressing smiles, laughter, grimaces. Emotion pulsing just below the surface, thoughts of elsewhere already sparking in their eyes.

6.0

He pushes harder. Further. Somewhere. Who cares about the knees, ankles, chest, heart, throat. He never watches the TV, afraid he won't feel it when it all starts to break down. It's why he comes here, to look at his own face in the mirror when the burn begins, to see himself feeling something like pain. He punches the button to crank up his speed, 7.9, 8.0. Hard to breathe. He lifts his head to watch his reflection, when a sudden movement outside catches his eye.

The window cleaner spins his mop, then stops dead, rigid, with the wooden handle by his side like a soldier with a rifle. He puffs out his bony chest and salutes hard at Mark, and then crumples, hacking, hands on his knees.

He looks up long enough to spit a slick of brown phlegm at the window.

Mark trips, heart seizing, his arms flying up to grab hold of something, anything.

"Buddy—you okay?"

His elbows slung over the safety bars, tips of his runners dangling off the back of the belt, a stranger's hand on his sweaty back.

"Yeah, yeah." Dizzy, patches of black. "Yeah. I'm good, man."

"I pulled the cord," the tattooed runner says as he helps Mark back to his feet. "You need a licence for this thing." An ink serpent coils around his neck, forked tongue flicking at his earlobe.

"I'm good, thanks," Mark says, collecting his water bottle from the treadmill's console and his iPod from where it fell. He glances back at the window. The man is gone, the spit wiped away. In the mirror, his eyes meet those of another runner, a ponytailed woman in her early twenties, the only face looking up from the televisions. The corner of her mouth creases in an almost-smile of empathy before she averts her gaze.

He doesn't bother changing. Just gets his things from the locker and wipes down his red face with a bleach-smelling towel. He tosses it in a bin on his way out the door, fishes for his keys in his gym bag. He's nearly at his car before he notices the window cleaner is there, leaning on the hood, waiting.

"Get out of here," Mark says, sidestepping and stumbling

off the curb. The man holds up his hands in surrender, in mock apology. "Seriously—leave me the fuck alone."

Mark slides into his car and pulls a fast U-turn to get away. Something smashes though his windshield like a javelin, detonating an instant web of cracked glass. The end of the mop sticks through the hole. Mark loses control, his car careening toward the sidewalk, hurtling toward the man.

"Can you hear me?"

Elise?

"Look at me if you can hear me. Turn your eyes to me."

She is there. She is beautiful, her hair aglow in coloured light. "Elise." His mouth is smushed into a plastic pillow.

"Don't try to talk, just look at me for now. Keep your eyes on me."

Her eyes, such kindness. Such love. Where had it been? He lets his head flop to the side so she can hear him. "Don't go."

She smiles in that way she does when she doesn't want to but can't help it. He smiles back. It is going to be okay.

"I'm not going anywhere. We're going to get you out of here."

There are lights all around. He closes his eyes, just for a minute.

"Stay with me," she says. "Stay with me."

He wants to say he will. When he has the energy he'll say he will, he'll say he can already feel the thaw. He opens his eyes.

"You hit a pole. You were at the gym. We think you might have blacked out."

"Elise . . ."

"Is that your wife, sir? Elise? Your girlfriend? Don't worry—you're alone. No one else is in the car. No one else was hurt."

He smiles.

"Sir, stay with me. Can you feel anything?"

Yes. Everything.

"Anything?"

A tear runs off his airbag.

"Sir?"

Yes, officer. Yes. Every fucking thing.

MOMMYBLOGGER

"Katie?"

I stop digging through the mess in the stroller basket and look up. Hovering over me is the silhouette of a man, a business-looking man, haloed by the February sun.

"Jesus. It is you," he says.

I stand, banging my head on the handle, and start to sweat even though it's minus fifteen. Drops roll down the sides of my face from beneath my tuque. For a flash of time I consider looking stunned and saying *Que?* then running down the sidewalk as fast as I can go. But there's no escape.

"Dev! Wow." I can't look him in the eye so I squint as if the sun is too bright and stare down at my mittens. They're quivering. "It's got to be what—ten years?"

"At least." He takes a swig from his Venti Starbucks cup. "Hey! Is this your little one?" he says, crouching down to peer through the plastic wind cover. He's tanned, like he just got back from three weeks in Maui. "Cutie. She's three, four months?"

"He. Five. Almost six months now, I guess." My heart pounding, words catching in my now dry throat. "Born in August."

"Good for you getting out in this damn cold," he says, standing up again. "My wife went bananas stuck inside with our first over the winter."

"Yeah, it's not hard to do," I say too fast, too loud, while making my eyes go googlie and twirling my finger by my ear. It doesn't work the same way with mittens, so I drop my hand to my side and say, "This—Felix, I mean— he's our second. I guess I learned about the crazy part the first time." I try to laugh casually but it sounds more like I'm about to hork something up.

"Nice, nice," he says. "Yeah, we have three now. Youngest in preschool. It's nuts. Just nuts." He smiles at the baby, then glances up at me just as I'm trying to read his face for signs. I look away and roll the stroller back and forth as if Felix is crying inconsolably, even though he hasn't made a sound.

Nov 29 | YOU ONCE SAID YOU WOULD MARRY ME

OR WAS IT COULD? YOU WERE LEANING AGAINST THE POOL TABLE AND I WAS STANDING BETWEEN YOUR LEGS.

It was still early. The bar was dead. The owner was playing against the bouncer, a $20 bill by the side pocket. You were saying how you were going to marry me/a girl like me. We couldn't say more than that then because we were both with other people even though we were essentially in love with each other. I rolled my eyes, but really I wanted to drop my head against your chest and rest there for a while. Billiard balls clacked, Radiohead played over the speakers, and the DJ in the corner flipped through CDs with his back to us all. The owner and the bouncer pretended they didn't see us, the same way they pretended not to see us at the end of each night when we slow-danced to Wild Horses.

"So, what do you do now?" Dev asks. "Besides this. Are you on mat leave from somewhere? Fancy lawyer or something?"

"No, no. Well, I mean, I was. I mean, not fancy but yeah."

"You're a lawyer?" His eyes widen and his head jerks back as if he were struck by a sudden strong wind.

"Oh. No. I didn't hear that part. No, I worked, though. Marketing, mostly."

He nods, loosening. "Nice. Nice."

"I mean, after this one, after Felix, it was just like, you know, we thought . . ." I stopped, trying not to sound defensive or apologetic. "I mean, I write now. Mostly."

Dec 2 | YOU CAN SAY NOW THAT YOU NEVER LOVED ME
BUT I KNOW YOU KNOW THAT'S NOT TRUE BECAUSE OF THESE TWO OCCASIONS:

1. When we were standing behind the bar and I turned around to grab a Keith's for someone and my face in the beer fridge light made you say, nakedly, "You are so beautiful." Even though my hair was in pigtails and your women were always so elegant. You were caught off guard.

2. That time after work when we were smoking in your car and I
   told you how lonely I was. I was looking out the windshield. You
   were looking at me. I had to tell someone and you were the only
   one I could. You drove me to the streetcar stop because it was
   raining and I didn't have an umbrella. It was 3 a.m. You told me
   that no one had talked to you like that before. I took it to mean
   honestly. I think you were affected by what I said because when
   you walked into the bar a week later you looked at me with the
   same new eyes you'd had when you drove away.

"A writer! That's awesome. Good for you! Living the
dream, eh?" He nudges me on the shoulder with his coffee
cup. No real contact, no touching skin, but still I swallow
as some old sense memory squirms to life, the shadow of
desire shaking off the dust.

"Like for magazines?" he asks. "Oh wait, I bet you're a
novelist! I could see that, I could see that." He nods slowly,
taking me in with another new perspective. "I'd love to do
that one day, when I get some real time. Take a few months
off when the kids are a bit older, hole myself up at the
cottage with a couple cases of Scotch." He sips his coffee
then nearly spits it out. "Yeah! Like my wife would have
any part of that!"

His laugh is so easy. I smile and clear my throat as I
wipe my dripping forehead with the back of my mitten,
which isn't absorbent and just smears sweat across my face.

"Yeah," I pretend-laugh along. "No, not novels. More
like, personal stuff. Mostly."

Dec 5 | REMEMBER THAT NIGHT YOU DROVE ME ALL THE WAY HOME?

WHEN WE TALKED ABOUT THE SEX WE WERE HAVING WITH OTHER PEOPLE?

Whew! Even now when I think of it. Holy mother in heaven.

Face-straddling, headboard-clinging, tongue-thrusting detail.

One-upping each other the whole way along the highway as you drove. You let out a moan at one point, your hand over your mouth. Can't believe you didn't crash us into the guardrail, but it wasn't like you to lose control.

We didn't do a damn thing about it when you shifted your car into park in front of my apartment. You were quiet and I was dizzy. I said "Thanks for the ride" and then nearly fell down the steps to my front door. Couldn't get my key to go in.

How long ago was that? 15 years? How did we not lunge at each other over your console? How did we not just say Fuck it and pull up behind the Food Basics? The guy I was with then was a total loser. I should have said Fuck it. I should have brought you inside.

That was the hottest drive of my life.

"Personal stuff? Oh! Like a blogger!" He's smiling like it all makes sense now, like he should have known from the start. "My wife started writing—well, *blogging*—when she was off too. She loved it. Just getting all that stuff off her chest about being a new mom, you know?"

He sips his coffee, smirking. It must be frozen by now. I hope it's frozen by now. I jerk the stroller back and forth until I realize I could be giving Felix brain damage.

"She even took a class. One of those, you know, 'get out of the house and be creative' things for moms? For her it was really . . . what's the word?" He looks up at the sky as if it's a giant dictionary. "Cathartic? Yeah, cathartic. Like she'd exorcised some evil spirits. I could see it in her eyes when I'd come home. She'd got it all out of her. All the shit you guys have to deal with."

Dec 9 | ARE YOU STILL WRITING? YOU ONCE TOLD ME YOU WERE WRITING STORIES

SOMETIMES I THINK OF HOW, IF WE'D GOTTEN MARRIED, HOW WE'D SIT BY THE FIRE AFTER SEX ON SNOWY WINTER NIGHTS AND READ OUR STORIES TO EACH OTHER, SIPPING ON EXPENSIVE RED WINE.

You'd be a good critic. Good-humoured but honest with me. You would challenge me. I'd sit with a pen and only be a little pricked by your criticism as I listened and nodded and crossed out and circled things, writing pretend notes in the margins. You'd stroke the dog's head absentmindedly with your free hand, the one not holding my stapled-together pages, your feet up on an ottoman, your brows furrowed.

I'd probably be a little more gentle with you because, let's face it, you don't have that much time to spend on your writing with your finance job that keeps us in such a nice house with a real stone facade and a wood-burning fireplace. But I'd be unprepared for some of the good stuff that would come out. The real scraped-away honest stuff that makes your voice tremble as you read it out loud. I'd nod and drink my wine as though thinking very hard about a particular turn of phrase you used and the crackle of the fire would be all there was between us. We'd watch the fire until eventually I'd say something to try to mask my envy, which might come out as anger about something unrelated. Like how you're always leaving your plates in the sink for me to rinse and put into the dishwasher when it's right there. I'm not your maid. Or your mother. She did too much for you. I might actually get angry about it then and have to walk away.

I'm sorry about that.

"Cathartic," I repeat as though mulling it over. "Sure. It's cathartic for sure."

I consult a pretend watch at my wrist, which, even if it did exist, would have been covered by several layers of winter clothing. "Oh geez. I have to get back. I have someone coming to look after Felix. I have an appointment."

"Sure, of course. I know how busy things can get for you guys. Don't mean to hold you up." He moves his arm and for a second I think he's going to pat me on the head. Instead he squeezes my shoulder through my parka. "It was so great to see you, Katie. I remember those nights at the bar. Just barely now—like it was another life. God. Like a life someone else lived, know what I mean?"

"Yeah, totally. Another life. I know exactly what you mean," I say.

Dec 12 | I MISSED MY CHANCE. I KNOW WHEN IT WAS NOW. SHIT.

SHIT SHIT SHIT.

Remember the time you came by the bar to say hi, months after you stopped working there?

You were with some short dark-haired girl. I didn't get a good look at her. It was a busy night. You and I were yell-talking over the music and the crowd, leaning in close over the bar. My hair was piled up on my head in falling curls. I wore a short black dress and high boots. I was feeling good that night. I rolled my eyes at my annoying co-bartender and you smiled. Dimples. I had to get back to work. Five deep, the people around the bar. In the weeds, we said. When you were leaving you put on your coat and held your hand up to your ear like an imaginary phone. *Call me*, you mouthed from behind the girl.

I guess I must have been near some kind of happiness then because, anyway, I didn't call. So I missed my chance.

Is that the girl you married? Was that Kaia?

"Really good running into you, Katie," he says, looking right at me, before tossing his empty coffee cup in the garbage. He shoves his hands deep into his pockets as though he's just realized how cold it is and looks at me again. "I mean it. It's so great to see you."

He holds my gaze for a second and I imagine I see some kind of plea. And then, for the first time that morning, Felix lets out a wail, saving us all.

Dec 17 | I THINK I SAW YOU WALKING ONE NIGHT

A LONG TRENCH COAT FLAPPING OUT BEHIND YOU.
Such a businessman. And so handsome. Chiselled, people would
say, but still with a real glint of life in your eyes. It was years ago
now and it must have been fall because it was dark but not that
late; I had just finished work and was heading for the streetcar.
I stood at the corner, not crossing. I didn't want you to see me.
You were looking straight ahead and not around you, as your
tribe is wont to do. Striding straight ahead to some place
where someone was waiting for you (home, I assumed; some
swank loft with high ceilings and low furniture), briefcase in
one hand, a just-bought bottle of red in the other. I can't confirm
that part because it was tucked in a brown paper bag, but
I'm pretty sure that's what it was, a good bottle from the
Vintages section. Just an ordinary Tuesday night. Nothing
around you seemed to matter. You were happy to be going
where you were going, striding away from the rest of us. You had
stories to tell to someone you loved for the time being. I stood
heart in throat and watched you pass and didn't say "Hey! D—!
It's me!" because that would have been so casual and breezy
and in no possible way could I be either of those things. I'm
not good at being casual to begin with, and certainly not under
those circumstances.

I stand at the corner praying for the light to change,
the impression of Dev's body still lingering against mine
despite the bulk of our coats. He hugged me tight when he
said goodbye, and held on a beat longer after I'd dropped
my arms.

I pull out my phone. Three missed calls from Mitch.

I slip it back into my coat pocket as the light turns green, and set off for home, bracing against the wind.

Dec 26 | SOMETIMES WHEN I'M DOWN AND OUT AND WONDER WHAT COULD HAVE BEEN

I THINK ABOUT TWO THINGS:

1. The way you looked at one of your old girlfriends as she danced by the bar. She was blond and so obviously putting on a show for you and you were eating it up. While you watched her, ravenous, you told me that she was a Tae Bo instructor and had killer abs.
2. I will never have abs. None to be talked about in an admiring way with another person, behind a bar. And I think that would have mattered to you.

The front door opens and a blast of cold air reaches us on the living room floor.

"Hello! Hello?" my mother-in-law, Carol, calls from the hall. Felix sits propped by couch cushions beside me, turning a knitted monkey over in his hands.

"We're in here!" I call back, not getting up.

"Jesus, the fucking snow," she yells. "Almost broke my neck on the walkway. Not your fault, I'm not saying it because of that. I know you can't go out and do it now, with the baby I mean. No one expects you to! It just came down fast is all." Her voice gets lost as she bends over to untie her boots, the scarf still coiled around her mouth.

Felix looks at me with big eyes. I make a face that is

meant to be reassuring but his expression morphs from uncertainty to alarm.

"Do you have salt?" Carol calls out. "I can go put some down, in case the mailman. They could sue. Not that I think they would! You can't be the only one who hasn't shovelled. I was out front at my place at seven this morning so I could clear a path and lay the salt and still make the 803. I'm not saying you should. I don't have babies. I'm just saying that it's a process and not everyone can so I'm sure you're not the only one. The mailman can't sue everybody!" Her laugh gruff, her throat still recovering from the cold.

"Hold on now! I see it . . . there's a bit of salt left in this bag. Okay. Wait a minute." She grunts as she yanks her boots back on, a current of arctic air chilling us before the door slams shut once more.

Jan 1 | I'M SORRY I MADE OUT WITH YOUR BROTHER INSTEAD

(SEVERAL TIMES.)

I'd go to his loft at the end of the night, when he was in town. There was this one time he put his hand under my skirt and went to touch between my legs but he just ended up rubbing the crotch of my tights because they were too short for me and about 3 inches away from my body. He kept rubbing anyway. I don't think he noticed.

I guess by then I figured it would never happen between you and me. Before we were make-out friends, I'd ask him about you and he'd say things that meant you were off the market. I thought of you the whole time though. Is that sick? He was as close as I would ever get. And everyone always talked about how hot he was, which was true, but he wasn't you. Still, I went back there after my shifts for a time. He'd lead me past his buddies who were always there playing Xbox in the fluttering dark. A single strand of Christmas lights draped over the dresser in his room.

I've seen him a few times since. He's always so warm and friendly, telling me how great I look. I don't mean to, but I usually ask about you too fast. Sometimes it'll be mid-hug and I'll be released from his lean arms and his face will have changed. I take it to mean that this is a question he gets often and that maybe he was your proxy for other girls too.

"He's great!" He told me not long ago. "He's got kids now. So really good. Really good."

I've got kids too. A toddler and a baby. Boy and girl, so a perfect family.

It's amazing, isn't it? The joy?

Felix rolls over and hits a button on the musical frog. Digital Mozart. Piano Concerto no. 21, "Elvira Madigan." I only know that because I Shazam-ed it when it was playing one time and was surprised that it worked. The song is now nightmarishly out of tune, the frog terrifying as its eyes light up purple then blue then green to the warbled melody. I'm adding batteries to my mental list of what I have to pick up this afternoon, when the front door opens and closes again. I tense against the frigid blast.

"Okay! It's done. It wasn't so bad, the ice underneath. Where we are we have to go at it with a chisel!" Carol's taking off her coat now, unwinding her scarf that's wrapped four or five times around. I knitted it for her the Christmas I got engaged to Mitchell, in yarns of orange and yellow. She says it makes her think of sunshine and summer all winter long. It makes me think of that fall I made it, when Mitch and I sat on the couch drinking Merlot and binge-watching *The Wire*, cigarettes burning on the chipped bread plate we used as an ashtray. Creeping to bed in that old apartment with the stuck kitchen drawers and cracked bathroom tiles. All the sex, in all the rooms.

"No lawsuit now!" She laughs loud and turns with her arms already extended to take the baby from me. He is rooting, bobbing his head on the faded Beaver Canoe label at my breast, but she takes him anyway.

Jan 9 | I GOOGLED YOU

TO SEE YOUR PICTURE.

There's one beside the announcement of a recent promotion. I saw the building where you work. I now know you're on the 38th floor because it says. I also know your extension and the number of your executive assistant. I imagine your office has windows and I can see you rotating in your leather businessman chair to look out over the darkening city. Your fingertips tap against each other as you consider an important merger. Check that—your fingertips tap against each other as you think about me. I realize I've only ever seen that world on television, because then I imagine it cutting away to the next scene, which is me, here. Sweatshirt and limp ponytail and leaking breasts, sitting cross-legged on the couch with my laptop. There should be a song playing in the background, something melancholy, as I turn to look out the living room window at a tree covered in snow.

You look different from what I remember, but I'm trying not to think about it.

My phone rings. Mitch's picture lights up the screen. He's wearing a straw cowboy hat and sunglasses with fluorescent green frames, the shot taken the last time we were in Mexico. I can't remember what year. We were laughing so hard when I took it.

I grab the baby back from Carol and tuck him under one arm as I head for the couch, lifting up my sweatshirt on the way. "It's Mitch," I tell her, as if to explain, answering the phone.

"Hey," I say.

"What the fuck? I've been calling. I thought something happened." Mitch's voice doesn't match his picture. My pulse quickens and my milk doesn't flow. Felix unlatches and looks up at me, then bobs again on my nipple, fussing, trying to stimulate.

"No. Your mom is here."

"Shit. Did you shovel?"

I flip the baby around to the other boob.

"Other people have babies," Mitch says. "You're not the first one. Other people can have babies and shovel the walk."

"It's shovelled."

Someone says something in the background, one of his crew. They laugh together. "Hello?" he says back on the phone, his voice bent now by a smile for someone else.

"Your mom is here, and I'm trying to feed the baby. Is there something you need?"

"Just wondering if they called."

"No. I told you I would text if they did."

Felix starts to wail.

"Shit. That sucks. I thought by now for sure."

"Mitch, I gotta go."

"Yeah, yeah. Go."

"Wait. What time are you coming home?" I breathe deep, breathe deep. Put my nipple back in the baby's mouth.

"Can't say. Hard to know on a day like this, lotta variables. Why?"

"It's just. I could use some help here."

"Well I don't know when, Kate. Jesus. We've got this project. Delivery didn't come last night, so we're behind." He inhales. "Anyway, that's why my mom's there, isn't it? To help?"

"Are you smoking?"

"What? What's wrong with you?" He exhales, further from the phone this time. "Jesus. What are you, the SS? I've got shit to do, Kate. I know you do too, but it's like, I need to keep my sanity. Someone's got to stay sane in that goddamn house."

I close my eyes and take a breath. Keep the milk going.

"Anyway, what are you worried about? It's not like I'm smoking over the goddamn crib. Stay off Google. I'm not even in the fucking truck. Jesus, Kate." He inhales again, blows the smoke out like a heavy sigh. "I told you, the delivery. And plus they still haven't called, so what do you want me to do? Huh? I thought we were a team here."

Milk trickles down my flaccid belly, dripping from the other breast. I flip the baby back to that one, the phone gripped between my shoulder and ear. Carol unloads the dishwasher, putting bowls on the shelf for wineglasses.

Someone calls to Mitch again, wind in the receiver. "Oh, they're here? Fuckin' A. Babe—delivery just got here. I'm probably going to be late. I'll call. Love you."

I stare at the phone after he hangs up. Instead of throwing it at the wall, I tap the blog icon and adjust Felix on a pillow so I can type with my thumbs while he nurses.

Feb 2 | I DIDN'T THINK I'D SEE YOU

DIDN'T THINK WE'D TALK.

I took a detour after the baby's appointment this morning. Thought we'd pass your office on the way to the subway. Tempting fate, I guess. I'm still shaking.

You look good. Better than your picture—or, pic*tures*, I should say, because I've seen a few of them. I've seen a few of them because I've been to your house. I've been to your house because your wife invited me there. She's very pretty, Kaia. So pretty it's hard not to look at her. I caught just about everyone in our memoir-writing course staring at her at one point or another. That moms' cathartic writing class she took? I took it too, enrolled in the fall, after Felix was born. It was a continuing-ed thing at the university, though, not just for moms. Or women.

She's a good writer. Did you know that? It took her a few weeks, a few tries, but when she got real—whew! She wrote this piece about decorating your cottage, room by room. Sitting there by the big bay window with the view, listening to the designer go through a whole book of white paints while she touched a dozen fabric swatches spread across her lap, trying to feel something. The cicadas outside droning like air raid sirens, the Percocets she downed with a mug of vodka when the designer drove away. How she lay on the dock like a starfish, spiders crawling through her hair.

I told her how much I liked it, after that class, how vivid it was. We talked about kids, about writing. She asked me over. I brought Felix with me—my daughter's in preschool, too. He was still so small and could sleep anywhere. She served cappuccinos and biscotti and when she went to get napkins, I got up to look at her wedding picture on the gallery wall.

I didn't hear her come back in, didn't hear her next to me. Think I was in shock. She said some things about updating the photos, about it being on her list of things to do, about what I must think after hearing her stories.

I couldn't take my eyes off you. I was in your house, your living room, breathing your air. I was sucked into a vortex of spinning memories: laughs behind the bar, whispers by the pool table, our bodies pressed together for late-night slow dances, feigning innocence. I could smell the beer and the sweat.

I kissed her. I turned and I kissed her pretty, pretty mouth. Lips that parted, briefly, and let me in, the way they do for you. I kissed her the way I wanted you to kiss me so long, long ago, the way I want to be kissed right now.

Sorry, I said, when she stepped back. I said it again. I told her I was tired, delirious.

She said it was okay but she looked hurt. Disappointed. I think she wanted us to be friends.

I couldn't get you out of my mind. Something woke up when I saw your face, when I felt her loneliness. Maybe you were lonely too. Maybe we both took a wrong turn. That night, after a 3 a.m. feed, I opened my laptop and yelled into the dark the only way I could. Writing to you was like a bridge out of here, a lifeline flung through time, a middle finger flipped to my shittiest, loneliest days.

The phone dings, a text from Mitch.
Def late tonight. Wrong delivery.
Told Steve would grab a beer after.
Rough go with his wife. Will call. Lv u
Felix has fallen asleep, his suction loosened, his mouth still near. I keep typing.

And then there you were. Here you are. On the street, in a coat and shoes and a scarf knotted just so, with eyebrows and nose hair and a self-satisfied smirk while a wife in despair echoes all around you. Close enough that I could smell the cologne and hair product and dry-cleaning chemicals which don't at all resemble the sweet sourness of our T-shirts at the end of those nights, your breath in my ear, my nose in your neck.

Maybe you are lonely, or maybe you're not, either way it doesn't matter because you're not the You I built from old memories and new disappointments.

And, besides, if it was you and me instead of me and him and you and her, I might be writing this shit about him because then he'd be the one that got away.

Felix stirs. I put the phone down and lift him up so his head rests heavy on my shoulder. Complete surrender. It is sometimes my most favourite thing in the world. I look out the living room window at the snowy tree against the February sky, but there's no song playing, no camera doing a slow pan away from high above to mark the end of the episode. No cutting to a black screen with white credits.

Carol dries her hands on a dishtowel and comes to take Felix. I resist.

"Aren't you going to rest? I'm here to give you a break. Go. Go now."

The landline rings and the call display shows it's the call Mitch has been waiting for. I let it go to voicemail so he can hear it first. I gently pass Carol the sleeping child and go to the kitchen to put a bottle of Prosecco in the freezer so it will be cold when he gets home, so we can celebrate.

WHAT HAPPENS

Lilacs.

I'll start there.

It was as though, all at once, every yard on our street had a lilac tree pushing through the chain-link fence, trying to catch my sweater or brush against my face as I walked past. I held my breath and looked down at the sidewalk, but I could still smell the bloom and the whole inside of my nose felt like it was being singed with a match. Spring.

It's hard to remember a time when it wasn't that way. But it mustn't have bothered me long ago when Mom cut clusters off our bush out back with the dull kitchen scissors, twisting and tearing the stubborn green marrow before wrapping the raw stems in a crunch of tinfoil. My fingers smelled like wet metal by the time I got to school and handed the drooping purple blossoms to whomever they were for—Mrs. Philips, Mlle Poucette, Ms. Bukowski, the librarian. The flowers sagging in a tea-stained mug by the blackboard for the remainder of the day, despite the quick blast of tap water they'd been given. That's another thing about lilacs. They never last long, after they've been cut.

It was around the time the lilacs bloomed that Mom aired out the house, snapping up blinds and yanking hard to lift the old living room windows. *Just a bit more air, a cross breeze. Feel that? There. That's what we need.* She used to wedge heavy books between the frame and the sill to keep the sashes from crashing down on our fingers while my sister and I examined the corpses of flies that had mummified over the winter. Hardcovers, library discards mainly, old mystery novels with plastic jackets that crinkled in the breeze. Rejection stamped in red across the top edge of the pages. DISCARD. Mom must have thought we were looking out at the street when she saw us there kneeling on cushions, but really it was the flies that drew us, lying on their backs with their dead stick legs folded neatly against their bodies, tiny invisible rosaries woven in their grips.

She got rid of those books. Threw them all in boxes that she dumped by the sidewalk along with everything else she suddenly considered non-essential. I picked one up and smelled it when I came home and saw them there that day. Cracked its spine, inhaled and felt the sting of memory. After the books were gone, she used blocks of wood to prop up the panes, and sucked up the flies with the nozzle of her vacuum.

I began to hate the sounds that bled in through those opened windows. Honks and sirens and thumping bass and kids yelling as they ran by with basketballs tucked under their arms. The double-ding warning of a bicycle bell, the warbling music of ice cream trucks. But soon that all blended with the *ch-ch-ch* of sprinklers and the protests of seagulls and the crescendos of cicadas, stirred into the soup of summer noise. And summer was nothing but a hot haze of exhaustion after all that hating in the spring.

Sprinklers.

Always the same memory: us, lying still on top of the sheets in our cotton nightgowns, yearning for a breeze to waft in through the screen, listening to the beat of the sprinkler next door. And just when its rhythm began to lull us to sleep, it stopped with a squeak of a knob and the other sounds of summer nights rose up through the air. Crickets. Footsteps on the sidewalk in time to the jingle of a dog collar. Caustic teenage laughter, somewhere. A car approaching from far down the road, pausing at the stop sign, then accelerating with a soft drone. Lonely. Maybe not, but when it kept to the slow speed limit, it sounded like it had nowhere to go. We lay and listened and drifted, agreeing without words when it was time to fall asleep.

I saw the low moan of her name spray-painted on the back of a park bench near the school, not long after it happened. The A stretched wider than the rest of the letters, so you hear it drawn out in your mind.

SADIE

Nothing left. Nothing left to do but breathe in again. It was impossible to tell if it had been painted there before or after, or even if it was in reference to her at all, but I didn't know any other Sadies. It was easy to believe it was done by some boy transfixed by her white teeth and auburn hair that dried in waves on our walk to school each day; easy to imagine him with a shattered heart standing alone at night in the park, spray can in hand, the tip of his index finger blackened by his longing.

I like thinking of the boy like that. Feeling real things. It slices through the melodrama that overtook our high school when the news broke. I wasn't there, of course, but I knew what was happening—the dispatched counsellors, the assembly, her "favourite" song played over the PA system during the morning announcements (a weepy ballad she once said she liked; God knows who said it was her favourite). I could see the police arriving early that morning to speak directly to our principal, Father O'Neill, to tell him what happened, to ask him questions. His office door closing behind them, the younger officers removing their hats, uncertain of the measure of respect due a man of the cloth these days.

I didn't have to be there to know what it was like. When we were in grade nine, two years before, a twelfth-grader named Dwight Reid was killed in a car accident on an icy road. It was January. A Tuesday. On Wednesday, girls who never knew him were weeping by their lockers, waving away attempts at comfort as they ran to the washrooms in competing states of grief. Aidan Walker, who played baseball with Dwight, punched a wall and broke his finger and two of his knuckles, an injury that led some

American college to revoke his scholarship. He was a pitcher, I think.

The day before the funeral, there was a school-wide assembly with a slide show of pictures from Dwight's life, soundtracked by an instrumental recording of "Little Wing." That it was Dwight himself playing the guitar rippled through the crowd (*Oh! He loved Jimi Hendrix!!*), though that was never confirmed. And each photo projected on the screen—a Christmas-morning toothless grin, in the shadows of a cottage bonfire, on his concrete front porch in a beige suit beside Lisa Myers-Lincoln before last year's semi-formal—evoked its own murmur or applause, each picture more naked and naive than the last.

Lisa, his girlfriend, sat in the front row surrounded by a gaggle of sad-faced girls who fought to embrace her when she turned to fall into someone's arms. The friend she'd chosen stroked her hair and whispered in her ear and looked skyward for an answer, conscious of her current role in the spotlight, which, literally, fell upon her due to badly angled stage lighting that no one had bothered to fix. The others thrust clouds of Kleenex at Lisa, cooing and hugging one another in a tangle of bony arms and a cascade of dripping tears, carefully dabbing beneath their eyes lest their mascara begin to run.

Dwight's mother was there. Just for a short time. Long enough, I'm now sure, to realize that no comfort could be found in that auditorium. She had been sitting somewhere in a darkened part of the front row with Dwight's older brother, Dylan, who'd just graduated and attracted lingering gazes from the teary-eyed girls on his quick ascent up the aisle. Shortly after the slide show started, his mother got up and retreated to the back doors, clutching her brown purse to her body. *That's his mom! That's his mom!* the assembly whispered in waves, falling silent as she passed. Ashen. Someone handed her a rose, which she took without smiling, Dylan a few steps behind.

There was a part of me that wanted to be a crying girl in the front row. They were so pretty with their wet faces, so close to the epicentre of tragedy. Sadie had snuck out for a smoke by then. Bullshit, all of it, she'd thought. We'd begun to diverge around that time. I was still languid with after-school TV and *Tiger Beat* magazines; she was catalyzed by The Cure, Doc Martens, and friends with black lips. Further from me but, still, I could sense what she was thinking. Usually. Even if we weren't identical, we were still twins.

People watched her. She was beautiful, yes, but she was also intense and self-assured, her gaze solid and straight ahead. Always a few steps behind, I learned to expect people's eyes on her, men, women, other girls hot with flames of envy. Sometimes they'd catch me catch them and they'd look away, embarrassed, or briefly glance back with curiosity, as though trying to figure out what genes she and I shared.

I was sixteen when their eyes shifted to me, and usually only when they thought I couldn't see them. Months after it happened, I would walk by wearing headphones while they stood staring in their yards, leaning on their rakes, or they'd close their lockers as I passed and watch me as if I were a ghost floating down the hall.

That's her.

I wasn't floating, though. Each step felt like it was taken in knee-deep quicksand. I knew what they were thinking, what they were wondering.

What happens to. Now.

When we were in grade four, there was a quiet boy named Ramon whose twin sister had died at birth. We didn't find that out until he'd been at our school for a number of months, and when I heard, everything about him changed. An absence settled all around him. I could see it echoing, undulating, encircling him like a moat as he sat at his desk by the windows, drawing spirals in his notebooks or turning to look outside at the maples over the teachers' cars below. Mrs. Fitzpatrick would tell him to stop dreaming and pay attention and I wanted to tell her to shut her mouth. The legs of my chair screeched against the linoleum as I shifted closer to Sadie, who sat beside me then.

So, what happens to. Now.

Absence, yes. All around.

And.

The smell of lilacs on the breeze through the screen. Faraway rattling ramshackle aches, a barren plain once home to despair, tired heart pumping still. Some part of it indifferent enough to keep you alive despite. The deepest part, I think. A metal engine in a dark space far below the surface with pistons that pump and pump and nothing else.

They—someone—said to write. That it helps with. *It's been a long time, Rose.*

But there is no straight line anymore. Fragments now. Pieces to pretend to fit together.

Lilacs, the smell on the breeze coming through my bedroom screen. Men at the door, voices low. A howl from my mother who'd only that day opened all the windows to let in the spring.

I didn't go down, didn't need to hear. Before there were words to describe it I had been cut.

They opened my door and saw me there.

A girl wrapped in a crunch of tinfoil.

THE CENTRE

I once told Colette to shoot me when it comes time to put me in a home.

"I know you don't mean that, Mama," she'd said, cutting the stems off strawberries at the sink. She smiled, easy, and hummed some tune I couldn't place.

"I'm not fooling around," I told her as I laced my white shoes at the front door. "Find a pistol, point it at my temple and pull the trigger."

"Nice, Ma. Real nice image." She rinsed the strawberries in a colander. I stood back up, knees cracking.

"Hear that? Getting old. Can't have that much longer. Better yet, just sneak up behind me with the gun so I don't see you coming."

"You want any of these?" She turned, eyes wide and blue. The spit, right then, of her father. Funny, almost. You try and try to blank out the memory of the one you hate most in the world and *bam!* there he is, like a crack of lightning, in the face you love best of all. I turned away, pretended to rummage through my purse for my keys.

"Nah. I'll grab Timmy's on my way."

"Suit yourself," she said. Then, "Love you, Mama!" like she always called out when the screen door creaked shut behind me.

"Love you too," I called back, wanting to sing it with the force of a gospel choir, wishing I could spread out around her like wings to carry her through the rest of her life, her feet never touching down on filthy ground again.

Framed pictures on the walls of lakes and trees and sunsets, puffy vinyl couches, magazines fanned out on coffee tables—*Cottage Life, Chatelaine, Zoomer*. Like the people sitting around are just waiting to get a tooth pulled. None of that is fooling anybody. You know by the smell when you step through that door that they might be waiting on something, but it ain't the dentist.

I can tell you first hand, nothing makes that piss smell go away. Not even when we Pledge the tables and mop the floors with bleach. The odour hangs in the air day and night no matter what we do to keep the place clean. To keep the people clean. And this, one of the fancier homes in town. No way we could afford to live here even if we wanted to when the time comes. And I'd never let Colette put up all that cash for me neither, not when she could keep it for herself. Can't say I notice the smell much after working here the better part of ten years, but you sure can see it in the faces of the people who come to check out the home for their parents. Men especially. I see them stride up the sunlit sidewalk, all hopeful and determined, coffee cup in hand from the Starbucks down the block. You can almost hear the thoughts running through their heads as they press the buzzer by the door and take in the exterior:

This is good. A good place. Nice stores to walk to in the neighbourhood, to get coffee with her new friends. And we'll visit all the time, of course. It'll be even better than her apartment/house/cottage with the willows by the lake.

But then Lyle buzzes them in and the doors swish open, and the men, the sons, they step inside and get a noseful before their vision can adjust to the light. That's when you see their faces drop and their eyes flare. Guilt, sadness. That flicker of fear.

It's not long before they catch a glimpse of the holy trinity—Lois, Henry and Mad Mary—all sitting in their wheelchairs facing the door like they do every day, waiting for someone to come take them home. Lois with her wispy hair set in curls, she does her royal wave, says, "Hello, dear, just looking for David. Was he out there parking the car?" Henry gives a stern nod like he means business, then sets his eyes back out the window, and Mad Mary, well, she can't say much anymore. Just lets her head sag over her shoulder like it does, mouth not quite closed, bony arms crossed over her lap. Hard to imagine now the whip she was not long ago, yelling at us all to go to hell, throwing tea-time biscuits halfway across the dining room with the arm of a minor-leaguer.

Strange what you miss when it's gone.

The look on those man-boy faces doesn't ever last long, though. They're barely inside half a minute before

Agnes is strutting out of her office, hand extended for a hearty shake, smile sparkling as though they've just boarded her cruise ship. The men straighten up when they see her, shoulders back, strong again, some kind of pride or relief rearranging their faces as they reach out to shake her hand. Vitality in her grip, a wink in her eyes. She knows, she understands, her face tells them, and you can see the new thoughts churning in their minds

This is the only option

tightening the grip

Really, it's the only thing we can do

of the wrench tugging at their guts.

It'll be fine. Mom will be fine here. Happy, even.

And with a lift of her arm like goddamn Vanna White at the puzzle board, Agnes points the way to her office, and the two of them disappear to the place where voices are low, decisions are made, and names are signed in ink here, here and here.

I've seen it enough times to know that the women-kids, they're different from the men. Almost like they know what to expect before the door opens. Like the smell of old-people piss is just one more thing to add to the long list of secretions they've had to deal with as mothers, as wives, as women. Peed on, puked on, shit on, bled on. I remember sucking phlegm out of Colette's nose when she was just a baby and couldn't breathe. Nothing more, nothing less than the way it is. Makes sense to me anyway, why the smell alone doesn't make their faces fall.

I'm not saying it's easier for the ladies. I see the way

some of them hesitate before pressing the buzzer, the way they adjust their purses on their shoulders, smooth out their hair with their fingers. The way they look at their reflections in the glass door, hard and still, not knowing that we can see them from the other side. When the doors slide open, they take in the room with a long, slow sweep of their eyes, heads nodding as though running through some checklist as they clutch at their purse straps like life-lines. Some of the women smile at Lois when she asks if they saw David in the parking lot, some say they didn't see him but they're sure he'll be there soon. They nod back at Henry and let their eyes linger on Mad Mary before their names ring out in the stale air, Agnes parading out toward them. They're already straight and strong, the women, so not much changes when they shake hands with the man-ager; it's only when they're back in their cars, seat belts buckled, keys in the ignition, that they crumple a little bit and let their heads rest down on the steering wheel.

Everyone puts on a good face, though, when they wheel mom or dad inside for the first time, chatting away about the facilities and the food and the views of the park and the spacious rooms, while mom sits there with wild eyes and folded hands, or dad with his chin raised in a heavy mix of pride and defeat.

Of course, that's not always how it goes. Just the way it's settled in my memory.

Colette was down with mono the week Bob and Sue-Ann Strallen arrived, so I wasn't there, but I imagine it was their daughter, Judy, who helped carry their things and led the charge in setting up their double suite. No nonsense, that Judy. Still running a law practice deep into her sixties, kids, grandkids of her own. A marathon runner. Straight grey hair cut in a perfect ruler line at her chin, the colour of her eyes to match. Not the kind to sugar-coat things, but then again, there wasn't much to sugar-coat when she moved them in here. *Lucky* was the word you heard a lot when it came to Bob and Sue-Ann. Lucky they still had each other. Lucky they were still in love. Lucky they weren't alone in the dark when the door clicked shut behind them at night.

Even I envied them. My Russell was no good from the start. Should have seen it long before I took Colette and fled, but fear has this way of casting shadows and whispering fantasies when the truth would be too much to bear. Then I found him standing over her while she napped that September morning, one hand pulling down his pants and, well,

Well.

Probably best he was so much bigger than me, so much stronger, best I couldn't get my hands on a gun, because he would have been dead right then and there and I'd be in jail and Colette would have had no one. Instead I wrapped her sleeping body in flannel sheets and took off into the black pit of that night, my way forward, our way out, lit by rage. Even now the hot white of that wrath, that terror, can blind me out of nowhere. Even now when I search her face, her movements, her words for some lingering nightmare memory, for some jagged scar he left on her, even now I could kill.

I never connected with anyone else after we left, what with shift work and my girl to take care of. Never had the chance, and never wanted it, I guess, after all that. Besides, Colette and I alone had love enough for twenty.

But, sometimes, when I see these grown kids wheeling in their parents, sister pushing the chair, brothers carrying the bags, when I see the hope and love on their faces, sometimes I think it would have been nice to have a normal family. A bigger one, with a good mom and a good dad and brothers and sisters and cousins, all those hugs and laughter and tears they'd churn out, all those hours that would turn into years' worth of memories to smile back on when you've got nothing left to do but stare at the ceiling. And, if you're lucky, someone there to lie beside, to describe each moment, when you can't remember much yourself.

Sue-Ann raises a shaky hand from her walker to touch the cedar sign that hangs from their door, *Our Happy Place* carved into it on a diagonal.

"Now that's a lovely thing, isn't it?" she says. She always says. "What's it for?"

And I tell her again (and again) that it was from their cottage, a gift from friends long ago on their twenty-fifth anniversary. She lets that settle in and smiles again, looking like she's landed on a memory. I'll admit that when the door is closed and there's no one else in the hall to see me, I bring my nose right up to the weathered wood and inhale. Pines, rain, dirt. I love that smell. I imagine that sign hanging by their grassy driveway under a canopy of breezy green, marking the end of a winding, hilly gravel road, the sun baking it greyish white with decades of summertime heat.

Slowly, we make our way back into her room and Sue-Ann pauses, as usual, to look at the cottage pictures that cover one whole wall like a gallery of joy.

"Look at that," she says, dentures clicking as her smile broadens. "Aren't they just having a ball?"

Black-and-whites of golden hour barbecues, of tanned shirtless men with cigarettes and stubby beer bottles, of bathing beauties lined up along the dock. Pictures of wet-haired grandkids huddled together in towels by the fire pit. Burnt noses, mosquito-bitten legs. Babies on the laps of aunts and uncles, in the arms of grandparents. Friends raising glasses up to the camera, eyes rinsed with laughter. Whole families lit amber, smiling at the setting sun. Empty wine bottles, cobs of corn, squeezed-out tubes of sunscreen, towels slung over the railing to dry. Look at that wall long enough and you're there, the tires of your car crunching up the gravel road to the sign that creaks in the breeze as you peer through the trees at the glittering lake just beyond the cottage. You can hear the kids screaming bloody murder, chasing each other around the grass, Sue-Ann yelling from the deck to *Slow down!* and *Be careful!* as they race to the dock, launching themselves one by one into the water with squeals and shrieks and a quick succession of splashes.

I could see Colette like that, in a place of our own, like that. Flying off a rope swing into a summer lake sparkling with sunlight, free and laughing. No memories, no worries, nothing but that place, that light, that shock of cool water.

"Oh, isn't that wonderful?" Sue-Ann gushes, admiring a blown-up Instamatic shot of a couple dancing on the deck.

"You two sure had a wonderful time up there," I tell her. "Look at your face."

She leans in closer, her nose almost touching it. Hard to tell if she's trying to get a better look or hoping she'll slip right through, back to that moment.

"Yes," she smiles. "What a time we had!"

Jazz used to tinkle out of their room all the time. I'd pass their open door a few years back, see her sitting in her pink velvet wingback with a crocheted blanket over her legs, her fingers tap-tap-tapping to the rhythm as Bob heel-toed his way around the room as best as he could manage, arms wrapped around some invisible partner, the ghost, I imagined, of a younger Sue-Ann.

"Judy coming today?" she asks in her wavering voice as I help her into bed. "She said she brought me a scarf. From Paris."

"I bet it's a beautiful one too," I say, tucking the sheets around her. "With her taste?"

"I hope she comes today. I could wear it to Betty's luncheon."

"You'll look just gorgeous."

She smiles, and for a second I see her as she was at fifty, at sixty, petite and confident, with a datebook full of lunches and bridge games. And then, with a blink of confusion, she's gone. A lost kid wandering a bus terminal.

I turn on the overhead TV and flick through the channels.

"Ah. Here's that artist you like. Look now, Sue-Ann. He's painting a sunset. Look how he makes those clouds with his brush. Makes them right out of nowhere."

Better to distract before she asks too many questions about Judy, before she starts wondering where Bob's gone. I used to think that people had a right to know the truth when they couldn't remember things, when they kept slipping back in time to summers and winters long ago when their kids and spouses were still alive. Thought it was unfair when we were told to just keep them calm, keep them happy, let them live in their worlds of warped memories.

I see it different now.

Sue-Ann watches the screen, her eyes fixed, her jaw lax. I bring the water straw to her mouth, let her drink, and put the cup back on the table. I pat the sheets at her knee and continue on with my rounds.

I could lie and say I'm like this with all the residents. You work in a place like this and every day someone's out to be hollering to you from their bed, distraught about one thing or another, remembering some baby that died eighty years ago, some teacher who whipped them with rulers, some uncle who slipped into the room where they slept with their sisters. Calling to you to throw them down the stairs, to hold a pillow over their heads, to hold their hand. Weeping, moaning, throwing shit around. Or lying there dead still just waiting for time to stop. Can't pay attention to all of it, can't let it get to you. Take that big gulp of air when you walk out the door at the end of your shift, drink it up like it's the first taste of oxygen you've had in a month, and dig to the bottom of your purse to find your car keys.

It's different with Sue-Ann. Has been, ever since Judy died. When I first heard about what happened, I thought it was a mistake. I thought she must have been just so damn tired what with being a lawyer and raising her kids and running marathons and worrying about her parents that she must have just pulled her car into the garage and fallen asleep right there in the driver's seat. I could see her shifting it into park and thinking, I'll just take a little rest, just for a minute, while I have all this peace here to myself.

Agnes had the centre's psychologist come in with the police to give Bob and Sue-Ann the news, to say it in a way that might soften the blow. Whatever he was supposed to do, though, didn't work because as soon as we all piled into the room, the cops following some old habit of removing their hats, Sue-Ann knew something was wrong. A rabbit with ears perked in the grass. They barely got a word out before whatever resolve she had gave way. I saw it coming and was there to catch her. Thought I'd have a stroke of my own when she collapsed—so wholly did I feel her pain, the shock of it. The very idea of losing Colette.

When the paramedics wheeled her out to the ambulance, one of the cops pulled Agnes and me aside.

"You should know," he said, "that Judy left a note. She included some details that we're investigating."

Agnes's eyes flashed. "Investigating. Into what?"

"Robert Strallen."

Agnes crossed her arms. I leaned on the wall. The officer said Judy had made allegations against Bob. He said they were old, decades old, but they were clear, specific, suggested what he called "a pattern of behaviour." He said they had to rule out that there were others. He meant children. He said other things but by then my ears were ringing and it was hard to follow what was happening.

I gathered myself as much as I could when he put on his hat to go, nodded when he said to get in touch if Bob or Sue-Ann said anything that could help with the investigation. I kept nodding as he handed us his card.

I don't remember much from the seconds after. Agnes walking with him to the door. The din in my ears, everything in strobe. Lyle reading a newspaper at the security desk. The kitchen door flapping open and shut behind me. The hallway sconces passing more quickly than usual on my way to the Strallens' room where Bob lay alone.

"Help," he called, lifting his head, desperate, like he was at the bottom of a well, like the fall had broken all his bones, like the walls were crumbling down. "Help me."

I couldn't move from the doorway.

"My chest." His breath shallow and rattling.

The wall, the pictures. I knew just about every face, every smile, every sparkle of sunlight by heart. Faces staring at me now as if from under water.

"Please. Help me."

The one I loved of Judy on his lap. Ten or eleven years old, hands on her knees, slouching, face turned in silhouette as she looked back toward the setting sun. His mouth open wide in a big laugh, his arm around her waist, pulling her close.

"Help—" It came out on a gasp. The flatline droned and in an instant I was there beside him, my hands doing what they do before I could think. I pressed the emergency button. I started compressions. I felt a rib crack. I exhaled hard into his mouth. I told him she left a note.

No one was surprised to hear he died that day. Everyone murmuring that nothing more than sweet heartbreak had killed him, when they saw how broken up I was.

Sue-Ann is sitting on the edge of her walker seat looking at the photo wall, hands limp on her lap.

"You should have called me to help you out of bed, Sue-Ann." I say, coming in from the hallway. "We don't want you to fall."

"Who's in this one?" she asks, looking at a picture of three grinning boys, sunburnt and piled on top of each other.

"Well, those are the Wilson brothers, aren't they?" I tuck in her bedsheet. "Phil and Audrey's kids? Cottage down the road?"

She looks closer, squinting. "Oh, yes. Of course. Aren't they just full of beans."

Truth is I have no idea who they are. Could just as easily have said they were cousins, or grocery delivery boys, or aliens who washed up on shore one Tuesday. I don't even know if it's Sue-Ann and Bob dancing in the picture on the deck, but that's what I tell her. I nearly tore the whole wall down the day Bob and Judy died, nearly smashed every one of the photos to the ground. I came close. But it wasn't my illusion to shatter.

"They look happy, don't they?" Sue-Ann says, pointing at the picture of Judy on Bob's knee.

I start folding towels, pretending I can't hear, assuming she'll change course soon enough.

But she keeps on. "Judy seems happy, doesn't she? Even though she wouldn't look at me when I took it."

I glance over, see her reaching out to touch the frame.

"She wouldn't look at me much in those days." She draws her hand back. "But, I suppose, I couldn't look at her either."

"Oh, now," I say, folding faster, breath catching. "Just teenage stuff, I'm sure. I know all about that."

"No. She was younger. She was a child."

"I remember when my girl was young," I tell her, trying to ignore the new quaver in her voice. "She could be a real handful."

Sue-Ann pauses a moment. "Are you married?"

I hesitate, put the folded towels up on the shelf. "Not anymore. Now, why don't we go down to the common room—"

"Widow?"

"No, I left. Now, I really think we should—"

"Brave. We couldn't do that."

I point at a picture on the side table, away from the wall. A deer in autumn woods. "Isn't that something?"

"We didn't do that." She's still looking at Bob and Judy. "They do look happy now. Don't they? Not so hard to see. Not so hard to believe."

Bile burns the back of my tongue.

"Where are we going?" she asks, looking around. We haven't moved. "I don't want tea. I'd like to rest my eyes and sleep awhile. You do what you need to, dear. Before we head out. Just need to rest my eyes. Long drive up and all."

I help her back into the bed, sweat beading along my hairline. I leave her staring at nothing beside her as I step back into the hallway and close the door. I reach for the wall. I try to catch my breath. I pull my phone from my pocket and touch her name.

"Mama?"

Her voice.

"What's wrong?"

Ah, Colette. My sweet, sweet girl.

"Ma. Listen to me. Close your eyes. Take a deep breath in. Like this. In," she says, slowing her words and inhaling deep, just like on the tapes she bought for me. ". . . aaaand out. Let me hear you breathe."

I slide down the wall. I try to ride her waves of breath. I keep my eyes open.

"Sorry," I say, when I can manage. "I'm so sorry."

"Stop. It'll be all right, Mama. I can come get you."

No, I say. I want to say. But I just sit. I just try to breathe.

"I'm right here," she says. "It's going to be all right."

But that's not true. That's not true at all.

"Yes," I tell her with all the breath I have. "Of course it is, my sweet girl. It's all going to be just fine."

A ROAD IN THE RAIN

It was the crack of her voice in the message that made me go. Raspy, sleepless. Asking could I please get the rest of the things she'd left behind in her hurry to get out.

It had been raining for days. Damp jeans as I slid into my car, fog blanketing the windshield. Cold air blasted from the vents of the old Skyhawk. I breathed into my hands.

His kitchen smelled of coffee and cat food, Caterina von Kittenburg performing figure eights around my ankles while I leaned against the counter and tried to look at ease. I had never been there alone with him. It felt like a different room, a different place now that it was his not theirs, even though everything in it looked the same. He was different without her too. Quieter. Humourless.

He took a pull off a joint and asked if I wanted some. Silky coils of smoke rose to the ceiling above us. I felt him watching me as I inhaled. I passed it back without looking up from my hand. He bent down into the fridge to find cream for the coffee, his movements athletic as he shifted the ketchup, the Coke, the leftover Thai food containers.

"Fuck it," he said, closing the door and opening the freezer above. He pulled out a frosty bottle of vodka, reached for two glasses on a high shelf.

He clinked his glass with mine. I drank fast, most of it at once, icy hotness lighting up the back of my throat. A few feet away he leaned against the oven, petting the cat's arched back with his bare foot. I stirred the last of my drink with my finger, made a comment about the rain to crack the air.

It wasn't all quiet. Cat von Kit's motorized purr. The chug and gasp of the coffee maker. Jangly music from a TV commercial in the other room, gay and bouncing. I'd seen that ad a thousand times, a smiling, peaceful wife, mother, alone, flapping out a clean white sheet over a bed in a sunny white bedroom.

I was picturing her beatific face when he closed the gap between us. His arm against mine, his glass clacking down on the counter. The tips of his fingers, then, on the back of my hand, barely,

barely,

before he took my drink away.

Old Spice deodorant, booze on his breath. His nose, my nose, his lips, our mouths, his tongue, rigid and cold. The cool damp hand that had held his glass slipping up under the back of my sweater, pulling me into him. Skin to skin. Goosebumps.

———

Two nights earlier, Kendra had picked me up on her way to their apartment to get her things.

"It's like a mutual letting-go," she'd said of their breakup, jerking her head to get the long bangs out of her eyes.

Unravelling was more like it. Unhinging. I could think of other words, but I kept quiet and smoked the one cigarette she said I could have in her sister's car that night, so long as the window was all the way down and my head was as far out as I could get it. I winced against slivers of cold rain and tried to shield the shaft of my cigarette, but it got wet in no time. Resigned, I tossed it, watched it disappear into a fold of black and turned my face up to the sky.

"What's the matter with you, Bea? It's fucking freezing."

She started doing up the window and I slid back in, my body pressed to the seat, knees to chest, shoes hovering above the leather.

"Christ," she said, blasting the heat through the vents and up the windshield, the fog that had formed receding in an instant.

When we pulled up to the apartment, I could see Dave through the front window lying on his couch, his face lit television-blue. He looked out toward the street, his gaze holding steady the slowing lights of our car. We were making eye contact but he didn't know, he wouldn't have been able to see me through the sloshing dark. He tucked the pillow further under his neck, when our car doors slammed shut and we made a break for the side door, his eyes drifting back to the TV.

He must have known that you could see right in from the street at night. The curtains wouldn't close all the way on account of the old rad beneath the window, so scenes of their domesticity played out for whoever was passing by. One of them—either he or Kendra—must have noticed at some point, coming home after dark to the other waiting on the living room couch.

I noticed.

I'd see them when I jogged through the neighbourhood, all the way to their street and back home again. It was a good distance, 5k there and back, which was why I used their place as a marker. Sometimes they were both there, stone faces in the shifting TV light, Kendra's head on his lap as he stroked her hair. Sometimes she'd be curled up like a cat with her legs tucked beneath her while she flipped through a magazine and he played video games, a bottle of beer, a glass of wine on the coffee table before them.

Once, I saw her back glistening in a shaft of street light, the clasp of her bra undone, straps sliding down her arms. Dave's bare knees pointing out from beneath her on the couch. Her black hair spilling down over both their heads like ink from a pot.

I followed close behind as she ran through puddles in the rutted laneway to the side door, her thin jean jacket pulled partway over her head. She knocked twice before shimmying her key into the lock.

"Remind me to give this back to him tonight."

"I have a feeling he won't forget to ask."

She stepped into the small, dark hallway and shook the rain out of her hair. I pressed in behind her and did a full-body convulsive shiver.

"Dave?" she called up the stairs.

She was about to pull off her jacket when our eyes adjusted to the dim light. Her stuff was stacked high in front of us. Hastily taped-up boxes, garbage bags leaking sweaters, crates overflowing with nonsense: cracked CD cases, waterlogged paperbacks, a used bar of soap embedded with strands of her hair.

I heard the hard clank of a jail cell door. Dave was watching *Law & Order*. No sign of him getting up from the couch to meet us. Only the cat at the top of the stairs, purring as she rubbed her plump side against the door frame. Kendra bent over and made kissing sounds, but Cat von Kit barely registered her estranged owner and sauntered into the kitchen, where kibble soon cracked between her teeth.

I lifted one of the crates, filled with magazines. *Us*, *People*, a couple of *Vogue* September issues, all of them two years old at least. I exchanged it for a garbage bag of clothes and heaved it over my shoulder. "Come on. Let's just get this all back to your sister's and go through it."

"Dave?" she called again.

"Just leave him."

"*Dave?* What is all this shit?"

I waited with her to hear the springy whine of the couch, the underfoot creak of the floorboards, a sigh maybe. Instead there were sirens and screeching tires. The detectives were pulling up to a crime scene. The cat, having finished her dinner, ambled past the doorway once more, back to the living room where her lone master lay waiting. Her curiosity must have been sated because she didn't turn to look at us this time.

I tried to quell the guilt rising up like heartburn. *This is just how it goes*, I told myself, *this is just what people do. There was always something between us.*

It was feeling good, for a second.

And then it wasn't.

Turned around, bent over, the edge of the counter grinding into my hips.

Hey, I said

(I think I said)

when he pushed my head down hard.

He yanked my damp jeans to my knees, shoved his hand up between my thighs. I lifted my head as much as I could. Rain streaking the windowpane. The screen torn and curled. His bike chained to a pole out back with a grocery bag tied around the seat to keep it dry.

He pushed my head back down again. I gripped the edges of the sink, my face too close to the tap.

"Hey," I said. I know I said. "Hey, wait."

He grabbed my hair and pulled. He took my breath away.

A few weeks earlier, we'd been in the alley behind the bar Dave owned, where all three of us worked.

"You're not into dudes, are you, Bea?" Dave said as he passed me the joint. He started to laugh, which made him cough on the smoke in his lungs, and he waved a hand in front of his face to compose himself. "What? Don't act like you don't know what I mean."

I took a tiny pull and passed it on to Kendra. "You're fucked, Dave," I said. "That's a pretty inappropriate question coming from management. Could call the labour board on your ass."

"So you admit it, then."

"I could see this," Kendra said on a deep inhale, gesturing back and forth between Dave and me. "You two would make a cute couple. Always bickering and shit." She shrieked as he buried his face in her hair and bit at her ear.

"You're both fucked," I said, taking the joint back from Kendra.

Dave kissed her hard on the mouth, then held out his hand. "All right, that's enough. Pass it over. You girls have work to do." He shook his head like a disappointed school principal. "Standing out here, smoking drugs on the job."

He licked his thumb and forefinger, squeezed the tip of the joint to put it out. "I mean it," he said, heaving open the steel door we'd propped open with an empty wine bottle. "Big party coming in tonight. All hands on deck, shipshape and the rest of it." He looked at his wrist to consult a watch that wasn't there and went back inside.

I lit one last cigarette.

"Give me a drag of that," Kendra said.

"You don't smoke."

"I do when I'm stressed. C'mon, before he comes back."

"No way. He'll burn me alive. Can't afford to lose this job. Economy and all that."

"He's not going to fire you, freak. Just give me a drag. One drag. I've got gum and body spray, he'll never know." She snatched the cigarette and took a long, elegant inhale.

She wasn't going to give it back. I reached into my pocket to light another.

"I'm late, Bea," she said, exhaling. "Like, by, a week and a half or something."

"Well, you better finish that smoke, then. I hear it's good for fetal development."

"I'm not kidding," she said. "I took a test. It wasn't negative." She took another long, nervous drag.

I swatted the cigarette out of her hand and snuffed it out with the tip of my sneaker. "Jesus, Kendra. No wonder Dave's all giddy-up and shit."

"*Dave?* Are you crazy? He doesn't know. And you're not going to tell him either." She looked away. "I've already made the appointment. I need you to take me there. Next Thursday."

"What do you mean, Thursday? What do you mean, he doesn't know?" I dropped my voice, even though it was impossible for Dave to hear. "What's wrong with you? I mean, yes, I'll take you. Of course I can take you, but you have to tell him. That's how this shit is supposed to go down. You guys crying, coming to some kind of under-standing. He's not a rapist. It's his and yours and you have some kind of duty to say something."

She turned her eyes to the sky. A star up there now. Or a planet. Or just a satellite.

She got quieter, almost whispery. "Yeah, well. I don't know if it is."

Hey Bea. It's me. Did you get a chance to swing by Dave's? No huge rush. It's just that I went looking for a sweater and real-ized most of my winter stuff is in those boxes. Shitty, eh? Heh heh. Probably should have thought of that when we went over there, huh? Aaaanyway. You're probably in the shower or something. Just give me a call when you can.

My phone ringing as he took me by the wrist from the counter to the couch without a word. The bossa nova ring-tone, the one she'd picked for herself on a dead night at the bar so I'd always know it was her.

Ringing as I stumbled behind, as he kicked his jeans off his ankles. Ringing as I told myself he was just intense, that soon he'd twirl me around and smile and kiss me, even as his grip tightened. Ringing as he shoved me down on the flattened couch cushions, as he clicked off the TV, as the springs whined and shrunk with his weight behind me.

Silence as I turned to look at him. His face sagging, gaze cold. Shadows in the dark. He slapped my leg. Again. And again with pain, without rhythm. Silence as he yanked my hips toward him.

Double-beep. Voicemail.

He pulled my hair again, jerked my head back. He locked his hands around my throat like a vise. Tighter. I couldn't breathe. Couldn't make sounds. I tried. I tried to say *stop*. I arched my back and scratched at his hands. He banged harder until he finally let go with a whimper.

A week earlier, she'd called and said, "Can you come meet me somewhere?"

Wind blew into the receiver, harsh static. I hadn't seen her since the appointment.

"What the hell time is it?" I sat up on the couch in my basement apartment, disoriented, the only light from the muted TV.

"I don't know, two or three, maybe?" She sounded drunk and like she'd been crying. "Dave and I—wait, there's a cab. *Hey!*" She whistled through her fingers. A car door opened and slammed shut. The wind-static stopped. She gave someone my address. "I'm coming over, okay? Dave kicked me out."

"Shit." I got up, wrapped the crocheted blanket around me and went to the kitchenette. "What happened?"

The fluorescent light flickered overhead, my arm in strobe as I turned on the kettle.

"He found out. He went through the history on the computer and saw all the clinic searches. First I said it was for you but he started grilling me and I totally broke down—I just couldn't hold it in anymore, you know? And he was, like, so mad he started screaming and shaking. Fucking whipped a beer bottle across the room and smashed it on the wall. Called me a lying cunt."

"Jesus."

"Yeah. So then I just let it all out. I finally felt like I was saying something real, you know? I said I didn't regret it and maybe it happened because it was supposed to happen. Maybe deep down I wanted to be with other people or something, you know?"

I switched phone ears and made my tea. "So what did he say?"

She started crying again, her sobs broken by a pause in the connection, someone calling on her other line.

"It's my sister," she said. "I just tried calling her. Hold on."

I went up the stairs to unlock the side door. My tea was half done when she clicked back.

"You still there?"

"Yeah, I'm here. Door's open so just let yourself in."

"Oh. Yeah, thanks, but I'm going to my sister's now. I'm sure Jimmy will be thrilled when he finds out I'm crashing at their place." She sniffled a laugh. "Anyway, you were right from the start, I totally had to talk to Dave. I think this is the best thing. Don't you?"

I sat down on the stairs and watched the mute television through the ornate wooden spindles. The tea I'd drunk would keep me up for hours. "Sure. I'm sorry you had such a rough night."

"Yeah," she sniffed again. "Me too."

———

He dressed in the kitchen, belt buckle jingling. Something tender in his voice as he mumbled to the cat.

My face felt flushed, wet and puffy. My wrist, neck, everything hurt. I avoided the street light that bled through the curtains, fastened my bra under my sweaty T-shirt.

He emerged, backlit by fluorescent light, his silhouette handing me the wadded-up ball of my underwear and jeans while he drank a glass of water. A loud series of gulps, a gasp. With nowhere else to go, I bent over to put on the rest of my clothes, fast as I could as he watched me.

He said I could fit the rest of Kendra's stuff in my car in one go. "No need to come back," he said.

I scanned the room for my bag. My keys were in the front pocket. I unstuck strands of hair from the corner of my mouth.

He told me to park in the laneway and went back into the kitchen to take a pull of his joint. He came back with an apple and my bag.

He said "Head's up" with apple in his mouth and threw the bag at me. I caught it, awkwardly, my keys falling out and chinking to the floor. I scooped them up fast, not waiting to find out if he'd reach for them too, patches of black starring my sight as I stood again on weak legs. He took another big bite, chomping the juicy mess with an open mouth. Air, spit, breath, pulp.

I tried to keep my voice still, tried to set it at a normal volume and said, "Maybe it would be faster if you gave me a hand?"

We avoided each other's swinging limbs, avoided each other's eyes, slipped into a rhythm as we loaded my car with Kendra's things. Him in the house, me at the car. Me in the house, him at the car. He started to whistle.

I saw only his untied runners, the worn carpet, puddles in the laneway until there were no more boxes, crates or bags.

I said *Okay, thanks!* or something like it and slammed the car door shut behind me. I glanced in the rear-view as I drove away, just as it began to pour. He was already back inside.

The wipers on full speed still not fast enough to keep up with the rain, the road a smear of lights. Blurry, clear, blurry, clear, my heart beating in time. I pulled over on a side street and lit a cigarette.

I jumped when the phone rang. Her picture on the screen: a red-lipped kissy-face shot she'd taken of herself. I opened the door in time to puke on the wet street, the rain washing it away in strands of stringy beige. I wanted to say something, so badly I wanted to say something, but didn't know how or what. I couldn't say *Help* because I'd let it happen. I couldn't say anything because he had been hers and I let it happen. I never said no.

I threw the phone in the back seat.

At some point I must have shifted into drive, must have pulled away from the curb, because here, now, is a passing slick of lights, the rumble of the street beneath me. My window open, my head out to take in big breaths of wet air. I know where I am headed.

The black awning, the high front windows he'd copied from a magazine. The sign, the name I'd thought was so cool. There, across the intersection.

My foot on the gas pedal, pressing down, hands clutching the wheel as they would the grips of guns. The clanging fantasy of what I want: to smash through the glass, the wood, the brick. To hear the shattering, the splintering, the crumble. Tables and chair legs cracking like bones as my car plows through the driftwood bar and destroys his wall of vinyl. The antiseptic tang of spilt vodka, rye, gin purifying the quiet that follows. It would look like an accident to everyone but him (the rain, my worn tires). It would be saying something. It would fuck him up.

But I can't.

There is rent to pay on Tuesday and no food in my fridge. There is not enough money to cover it all if I don't work this weekend, and there is no one to call for help.

I ease off the gas and tell myself that I'll make it through till Sunday. I'll keep my head down. I'll find a new gig next week.

But now I am skimming, weightless,

out of control.

I can't brake, I can't stop. There is no road for my tires to grip: only water, only rain, and I'm headed for the wall. I yank the wheel hard to the left to swerve away. Spinning, I brace for impact.

Rain on the roof, the windows.

Tap. Tap-tap-tap.

"Hey! *Hey!* You okay in there?"

A figure outside, knuckle-knocking, pulling at the door handle.

"Can you hear me? You all right, lady? Need me to call an ambulance?"

I roll my window down enough to talk. "No. Yes. I'm okay. I'm sorry. I just—I'm fine."

"You sure?" the man says, blinking against the rain. "You really spun out there. Didn't hit your head or nothin', did you?"

I will cry if I say more so I look down and shake my head no.

He lingers, glancing over at his running car, then back at me. "You sure you're all right, hon?" Sweetly. Ah, so sweetly.

I nod and turn up my lips in a brief smile, start my car again. I don't know where I'm pointed. He pats my window with his thick hand. Light sparks off puddles as he trots away.

I light a trembling cigarette and reach back for my phone.

Omw, I text. *On my way!* it auto-corrects, joyously. It sends before I can change it.

A set of headlights, now and then, as I go to her. Unseeable ghosts, unspeakable things, behind black windshields and frantic wipers.

She is under the shelter of her sister's porch, her arms wrapped around her for warmth. She releases a quick hand for a wave.

"Hey," she yells when I finally step out. "I called like twenty times!"

"Yeah," I say. "Sorry, I . . . I almost got in an accident."

"You what?" Holding her hand to her ear.

"An accident," I yell.

"An accident?"

"Yeah."

"You okay?"

"Yeah."

I carry one of the boxes up the steps to her. She takes it inside. I head back to the car for more, running to the porch and back again without cover. She comes out in a hooded parka to help.

"Cold, eh?" she says, passing me.

"Yeah."

We lock into a dance of our own, wordless, arms weighted then empty, weighted then empty, faster each time as we unload the car.

"Jesus, you look like Alice Cooper," she says, dropping the final bag into the front hallway. "You've got, like, mascara down to your chin. Come in and dry off. Have a glass of wine with me. My sister has some good shit."

"I can't." I back away, using my sleeve to wipe tears that look like rain. "Gotta work tonight, right?"

"Oh. Yeah, sure. Almost forgot. Well, thanks, Bea. I really appreciate this."

"Yeah, no problem!" I call out, and hurry back to my car. She stays on the porch watching me, the way you do when you want to make sure someone is safe. Or just to be polite. I stick my arm out the window as I pull out and give her a thumbs-up to let her know I'm cool, she can go back in.

I look up at the rear-view as I drive off. She is gone. The porch light blinks to life.

I have an hour before I have to be at the bar. No time for laundry. I'll have to root through the pile of clothes on my bedroom floor to find something clean and decent to put on, something dry, something clean enough.

INTERS ECTION

I.

Even in the middle of the day, even with its big warehouse-sized windows that lined one whole wall, that bar was always dark. Age and weather had permanently fogged the panes, allowing only a pale haze to reach the closest tables, the rest of the room in shadow but for the odd strand of Christmas lights slung along the black walls, and the candle flames that licked the smoky air from the mouths of wax-covered bottles. It took a few moments for Sebastian's sight to adjust as he shuffled in with his group, still engaged in debate from philosophy class. They'd talked loudly on the walk over, excitedly one-upping each other with remembered portions of theories they hardly grasped, their volume increasing when they stepped inside. Sebastian stopped mid-sentence when he caught the irritated stares of older students sitting nearby, their mouths releasing rings of smoke that stretched into silky O's in the drifting grey overhead. They sat in pairs or unselfconsciously alone with pints of beer and burning cigarettes, spiral notepads and second-hand books, watching as the boisterous herd arranged chairs and dragged tables together.

He looked toward the windows and furrowed his brow as though he were trying to unravel a very tangled problem indeed, doing his best impression of someone who belonged there. A man with matted hair read *L'Étranger* by the filmy light, a young professor or a kitchen worker on break, his leg bouncing with anxiety or thrill as he turned a page. Sebastian believed the people here had crossed into a realm he hadn't cracked, like the spines of the metaphysics books he'd bought in a manic rush that fall, and that now delivered only stabs of panic and reminders of his deficiencies from the corner of his room where they'd been abandoned in a heap.

Joy Division played gloomily from speakers hidden in the corners, briefly casting a pall on his group as they wriggled out of their coats, unwound their scarves and settled into their seats. He glanced at a foursome of graduate students drinking red wine from juice glasses, the music, he was certain, stoking legitimate memories as they murmured to one another with puffy eyes and a world-weariness he longed to exude.

The pretty girl from class took the chair across from him. Allie. He was surprised she'd come along. He'd narrowed his eyes at her in the lecture hall, and had expected she'd be gone by the drop deadline, so poorly did her glossy hair and pink lips fit with the rest of them in their blacks and greys and overall rejection of popular culture. She took out a lip balm and applied it, appearing to want to occupy her hands. She'd been quiet on the walk over. Someone ordered a pitcher and launched into a discussion on perception. Her eyes drifted from a spot on the table to the dripping candle wax and back down again as she listened, her straight blond hair falling against her face like two sides of a frame. Tenderness now cycled with the revulsion and lust and anger she ignited in him, along with the urge to reach for her hand.

The beer arrived and the guy who'd ordered it was now mangling parts of a theory he'd read or heard about in class and eventually worked it into another, more familiar topic that was better suited to his authoritative delivery. Something to do with colour-blindness. They realized one pitcher wasn't enough and ordered another and began speaking with heightened enthusiasm, proffering their own semi-formed ideas about sight and sound and comprehension. What it is to see. To hear. How the vibrations of tiny bones in the ear became music.

"Love this tune," a boy wearing an old tie over a T-shirt said, closing his eyes and nodding to "Love Will Tear Us Apart." He let the chorus play then asked, "What do you think that time was like?"

"It wasn't some paleontological era, man. It was the eighties." That from another student who only spoke when he could douse a question or remark with sarcasm. He smirked and took a long drag from his smoke.

"The early eighties, smartass. You were barely sentient, let alone privy to the discontent of teenagers on an entirely different continent."

"Do you have a point?"

"Do you believe this sound captured that time?"

"I thought I was too young to be privy to such discontent," he said in a surprisingly good British accent.

Allie laughed.

The boy with the tie rolled his eyes and asked the rest of the table. They questioned what it meant to capture a time with music. Had now been captured? Kurt Cobain? Eddie Vedder? That wasn't now, that was still before. They thought about it. A voice, was there a voice of now. Someone suggested that maybe it wasn't about capturing a decade or a year but rather a period in the life of a particular person. Maybe that was more significant and told a greater truth about a time. They paused, listening for their own plights in the nihilistic baritone. If they felt something it remained unacknowledged, though it seemed some were holding back, afraid, perhaps, of how their personal reflections would be received.

Allie coughed, then spoke up for the first time. Sebastian's breath quickened as the group turned to them. He feared she'd say something stupid. There was a poet she'd been reading, an Indian writer, she said, her voice trembling slightly. His poetry was heard in the tea fields in India, from the women in the fields. It moved her a great deal, and she asked what everyone thought was maintained in translation, what it was that roused something in her if so much was supposedly lost in the flight between two languages.

The others seemed to think about this for a moment, the smart aleck sipping his beer and grinning over the rim of his glass. The waitress brought nachos someone had ordered at a different table and Allie's question got lost in the confusion. Sebastian saw her eyes dip down again and he leaned in to ask what it was that had moved her. She said the words were simple and clear, as if there was no kind of dressing on them to trump up their meaning. She said she could hear music in them even though she knew none of the original language. She believed there was music in every language.

"But not the same music, you know what I mean?" she asked. Sebastian nodded as if he really got what she was saying. She looked so happy to be talking, to be heard. She was not what he'd expected.

Allie went on, pulling an extra-long cigarette from her silver pack on the table. "Do you think poetry in translation is a hybrid of the music of the two languages? A kind of symphony, maybe?" She lit it and blew the smoke out slowly. "Maybe that's why I was touched. Maybe it was a kind of connection, like a bridge or something."

He poured them more beer. Either he or she had then remarked on the similarity between music in very different parts of the world, the sounds of instruments in Ireland and India, for instance, and they got very excited at the realization of this.

Soon the voices in the bar multiplied, the late classes over. Students who'd been sitting alone with their notebooks and manifestos were now met by friends who let heavy knapsacks slip from their shoulders and thud to the ground. Another pitcher arrived. He grabbed it first and topped up both their glasses. She watched him, smiling, her eyelids heavy.

"Hey, did you ever see that Internet commercial?" he asked her, beer sloshing over the rim of the pitcher as he put it back down. "I keep asking people and they don't know it. The one with the little girl from *The Piano*? She was standing on the top of a mountain somewhere, talking about this thing that was coming, that was going to connect everyone. It totally freaked me out when I first saw it. It felt like a warning, like she was sent from the future to prepare us for the coming of something that was going to change everything."

Allie squinted at him as she smoked, as though trying to place it. "Hmm," she said, kindly. "I'm not sure . . ."

"Come on, you've got to remember. It wasn't that long ago. It was so crazy. It felt like some kind of international public service announcement. Intergalactic, even. I think she even called it the Information Superhighway." He searched her face for some kind of recognition. "No? Nothing? Man, just thinking about it still gives me chills. It was like it was supposed to be this exciting thing but her eyes were just, I don't know, kind of panicked."

Allie smiled at him, tapping an extension of ashes into the black plastic ashtray. "Was it for Netscape Navigator or something? Or maybe you dreamt it."

"No, no. I can't believe you don't remember." He shook

his head, smiling back in the candlelight that flickered now in true darkness. He checked his watch. He was supposed to meet someone. He didn't want to go.

"Hang on a sec," he said. "I have to make a call. Don't go anywhere." He got up and hurried to the hallway where the pay phone was. Third in line. He sighed and tapped the wall as he waited for the others to finish their conversations, wishing that he'd at least brought a pen so he could add to the names and song lyrics and expletives scrawled there, though he didn't know what he would write if he had. When it was his turn, he quickly punched in the number of the girl he was seeing, eager to tell her he was running behind, that he'd be a little late.

Allie looked up as he sat back down, his smile dissolving when he saw the bill on the table, everyone finishing their beers. He wanted to order another round for the two of them but before he could suggest it she drew a twenty from her wallet and said she had somewhere to be. He said he did too. They all put on their coats and scarves and dug change and crumpled bills from their pockets. They heaved their knapsacks onto their backs and ambled as a group to the station, hugging, waving, nodding in the direction of their respective subways, buses and streetcars. Sebastian and Allie lagged behind, not saying where they were headed. She tucked her hair behind her ear when she talked. Their arms were nearly touching. Most of the others were gone as they lingered on the platform not yet saying goodbye, the two remaining guys from their group exchanging rapid-fire final thoughts. Sebastian only got on his streetcar when it was about to depart, and turned twice to wave to her on his way up the steps.

He sunk into one of the single seats that line the windows, buzzing with beer and trying to hide a smile so real it hurt his cheeks. He looked back, scanning the platform, but couldn't see her anywhere. The doors closed with a gasp and the brakes released from the track beneath. The streetcar moved a few feet before it stopped again with a screech.

"Sorry," Allie said to the driver as she climbed aboard. "I forgot to give someone something."

She spotted Sebastian at once and went to him, a book in her outstretched hand. He reached out for it, their eyes locked as he took it, and then she turned and left.

In his memory she is standing on the platform, hands in the pockets of her coat, watching his streetcar pull out just as the rain starts coming down. He doesn't know if this is what happened or something he once saw in a movie.

He looked down at the book's cover. It took a moment to hear the rhythm of the syllables. Ra. Bin. Dra. Nath. Ra-BIN-dra-nath. Rabindranath Tagore. A collection of Indian Poems by the Nobel Laureate Rabindranath Tagore.

Pages were marked with red tabs. What she loved, he wondered, or what she didn't understand? What she wanted to return to, of that he could be certain. He turned to one.

> *It is the pang of separation that spreads throughout the world and gives birth to shapes innumerable in the infinite sky.*
>
> *It is this sorrow of separation that gazes in silence all*

night from star to star and becomes lyric among
rustling leaves in rainy darkness of July.
It is this overspreading pain that deepens into loves
and desires, into sufferings and joys in human homes;
and this it is that ever melts and flows in songs through
my poet's heart.

He read it again, then again, trying to hear the music—the symphony—she had talked about. He had to remind himself that the red tabs were there for her, not for him, that she had affixed them to the pages before she knew he even existed. But now they were his and he thought that he would have put a red tab on that page anyway. He made a plan to buy a pack of tabs just like them and from then on to mark pages in books he found significant too.

It was raining hard and he might have been in love by the time he reached his stop, his heart warm and thumping and explosive, but the girl he was seeing, whom he was supposed to meet at her house blocks away, was there beneath the shelter waiting for him with an umbrella. She popped it open as he came down the steps. She said she thought he might have forgotten his.

For a very long time, it was the best day he could remember.

II.

Sebastian found the book of poems as he was packing to move into his first condo. It had fallen behind a row of law textbooks, its jacket dusty and folded in half. The edges of the pages were bent on an angle, but two red tabs remained.

He clucked at the memory and opened to one of them. He read the first couple of lines, then flipped to the other tab. He remembered something about music, languages. So much noise in his head now. The din of constant anxiety since he'd begun articling, his moving to-do list, the dull hangover skull-throb from the firm's bonding event the night before. He leafed through trying to remember the name of the girl, what she looked like. He could see her eyes, the heavy lashes he'd mistaken for makeup, the way she looked at him, into him, when she'd handed over the book. The rush of feeling between them. He'd never forget it. Had he ever felt that with Petra? There wasn't a moment like that with her, ever, in their two years together, nothing that stood out. He could hear her in the kitchen sorting utensils. Their love was more mature, less mercurial. It was a good thing, he reminded himself, tossing the book in a box. *Even keel.* The stuff of a lasting connection. He was going to surprise her that night at dinner, he was going to ask her to move in with him.

The memory of the girl fluttered around him as he resumed packing. He wondered where she was. He played the moment on the streetcar over and over in his mind like he was nineteen again.

"What are you smiling about?" Petra was at the door, hand on her hip.

"Nothing," he said, startled. He looked away. "Do you remember that government commercial about the dawn of the Internet? The one with Anna Paquin?"

He hadn't thought about it in years. He stepped over boxes to his desk and flicked on his computer. He typed "anna paquin information highway" into YouTube's search box. In seconds it was there and it was nothing like he remembered. There was a mountain behind the actress and she was on the barren ground far in front of it. The landscape looked burnt, singed by the sun. She wore a black hat.

"There will be a road," she said. "It will not connect two points. It will connect all points."

Quick cuts. Flashes. Close and far.

"Its speed will be the speed of light."

Petra was over his shoulder. "Totally don't remember this."

"It will not go from here to there," Anna Paquin said. "There will be no more there." She skipped rope. "There will only be here." MCI Network. 1994. Viewed more than thirteen thousand times. There were comments.

He clicked the window closed and shut his computer down, unsettled.

"Weird," Petra said. "Kinda ominous, eh?"

No, it wasn't. Not the way he'd thought it was. It was a commercial for a company, not a PSA. He no longer thought that Anna Paquin had looked worried, or imagined that she'd been led into a room under tight security before the ad was shot, a bright white room with no windows where the few intelligence workers privy to what was coming let her in on the secret so she would look informed. It hadn't been like that at all. She'd probably had a private trailer and a folding canvas chair on the dried ground, production assistants milling about between takes with sandwiches and coffee and walkie-talkies.

"Yeah, totally," he said.

"I was thinking Thai tonight."

"Perfect."

"The usual?"

He cleared a shelf, letting the books crash down into an open box. She looked at him with eyes that said, *Was that necessary?*

"Babe?" her mouth said. "The usual?"

"Yeah, perfect."

He heard her efficient steps recede down the hall. He wiped the dust off with his sleeve, and moved up to the next shelf.

III.

There is a hawk perched on the edge of a roller coaster. It is winter and the amusement park is closed, dormant. Isolated. The hawk looks over the highway from its stead on the twisted metal rail, its feathers puffed and ruffled in the wind, its eyes watching the passing cars going through nowhere. Nothing here now between two places, the place you left and the place you're going.

Sebastian returns his gaze to the highway in front of them. "You see the hawk?"

His wife, Melody, would have had the perfect view, her eyes set out the passenger window for some time. "No. Where is it?"

"Back there. On the Wilde Beast."

"Riding it?"

He smiles.

Brown grass pokes up dead from snow that's not quite melted along the highway's edges. All the cars are chalky grey from months of salted roads, mud caked around the wheel wells. Plastic grocery bags blow torn and faded against rusted fences. McDonald's drink cups, empty cigarette packs, things tossed from car windows scatter the side of the road.

Children in back seats don't bother twisting their necks as they do in the summer to try to catch a glimpse of a coaster zipping through the trees or cresting an impossible height. They know enough to sense they too are nowhere now, and stare down instead at the devices in their hands that take them somewhere else.

The hawk's feet grip the rail at the top of a hill between the trees where the roller coaster turns, where the track bends on a slight angle to maintain the force required to keep the people safe. Vectors on paper decades ago to show the direction of the force at that precise point. It is where the bravest of riders raise their arms in anticipation of the drop, where gravity and speed and momentum compete for the chance to turn your stomach inside out. Vectors on drafting paper, long ago, playing inconsequential games with symbols scratched in pencil. The hawk watches passing cars from the oldest ride. Wood and metal and rickety. And there is only a bar across your lap to keep you in.

Wide white expanses fringe the park. A colourless sky, skeletal trees, wooden fences to keep cows and horses from straying onto the highway in summer. Evergreens too close to the roadside, frail arms now bare, poisoned by the exhaust from constant traffic, their fallen needles somewhere beneath the melting snow.

There is a hum in their car, the wind whistling through the door cracks, the whir of the engine. He's turned off the radio. Neither of them talks over the drone.

She turns as if to say something, stops, and looks back out the window.

"What is it?" he asks.

"Nothing. I'm just glad we're doing this."

He reaches for her hand over the console. She holds on a moment before letting go with a squeeze. Even her gestures have always been honest. Even when it's hurt him, he's loved her for it.

He puts his hand back on the steering wheel, the quiet between them not to be crossed right now. Something he wishes he'd known from the start. The tires of their SUV rumble beneath them on the pitted concrete, potholes to be filled in spring.

A patch of hotels spring up beige just after an exit, not close to any town. White space rushing past, hotels, white space rushing past. The dependable rhythm of the guardrail posts. Black removable letters on one of the hotel signs spell out **FRE E WI – F I.**

They are heading north for skiing and wood fires and bottles of wine, a weekend away, to reconnect. But, for now, they are here.

IN THE DARK

What was that.

A sound. Outside, by the door.

Paul?

Wait. He's in Ottawa. No. Miami.

Even farther.

I feel around for the phone I always keep in the bed when he travels, but nothing is there. Sheets and pillows, softness now stripped of comfort. A memory of plugging it in by the kitchen table last night, the battery dying in my purse before I got home. I rarely bother to charge it overnight like he does. Not until it's dead. He's good like that, preventative. On top of things. On top of someone else now, maybe.

A creak on the steps. Yes, that's a foot. A foot is slowly pressing down into one of the steps outside the front door, the weight of a body, the wood below buckling enough to creak. They're old steps. Should have been chopped up with an axe and replaced by a nice porch long ago. A couple of wicker chairs, a swing even. So many summers gone. If I'm alive tomorrow that's what I'm doing—I'm taking an axe to the steps. Paul can build the porch when he gets back. I don't care that it's February. But now a man, definitely a heavyish man, is standing on the creaking step, hoping I didn't hear.

I could run across the hall to the landline. I could sprint to the phone in the other room and dial 911. I could say—whisper—*Operator?* Yes, 15 Pheasant Drive. There was a sound outside, a creak. On a step beneath the door. The sort of sound made by a threatening sort of person. I can tell by the way he doesn't want me to hear him. Please send Emergency Vehicles.

No, this isn't an emergency yet. When she answers she will say: *Nine-one-one, what is the nature of your emergency?* I know that because it's what she said the last time I called, when I thought Paul had fallen down the stairs but it had actually been the ironing board. Or maybe that's the way the operator answers on TV and what I heard was some version of that question. There was the other time I called but I can't remember how she answered then because I was screaming and banging on the wall. Help, help, please help. Sometimes emergencies are obvious.

What is the nature of my emergency? Operator, I heard a creak on the steps outside the door. Please send vehicles with loud sounds and flashing lights. There's a good chance they could scare him away, so make sure the police are prepared for a foot chase over fences and through backyards to catch him if he runs.

I don't think 911 operators are allowed to laugh because anything can be an emergency. It's all relative. This one may not be an emergency *yet*, like calling 911 from the highway to report an accident just because a car ahead is swerving—but it could be very soon. *Imminent* is the word that comes to mind. This one could make the news tomorrow, after it changes state from Emergency to Crime to Crime Scene. When they put up the yellow tape to zone off the area and serious men in glasses wheel my covered body down the creaky front steps on a stretcher. A porch would look nicer, conjure more sympathy from viewers I think, what with the wicker chairs and such.

I could call Paul. Run on tiptoes to the phone in the other room to call Paul. He will answer his cell phone groggy in his trying-to-be-patient-with-you-Martha-but-I'm-really-getting-tired-of-this voice. 2:07 a.m. He'll say if you're really worried why would you call me in Miami. There is nothing I can do from Miami. I'm alone, Martha. He'll say, There is no one here with me. Please, Martha. Please. Go back to bed. And I'll have to quickly say that it has nothing to do with that and of course he's alone and so am I and that's the problem.

I'll ask him when this situation becomes an emergency. He knows that sort of thing, where the threshold is. That's why I have to call him. But then he'll say something about the sounds I always hear in the dark now and how the wind bangs the gate—The *wind*? What the hell do you know about the wind in Toronto? You're in Miami, Paul, you haven't the faintest idea what the weather is like here. And then I'll have to drop my voice back down to a whisper so the predator doesn't hear me, doesn't know I'm awake. There is no wind, Paul, I'll hiss into the phone. At least, the branches that normally make moving shadows on the wall are still. I will be home on Thursday, he'll say. Or whatever day he's supposed to come home this time.

I should call Paul.

There! Is he trying to open the door? Definitely something scratching against the glass, tugging at the handle. A hook. No, only in movies. A hand is scary enough. Paul will ask if I've taken my pills today. He'll say it with a sigh and look at his watch that he wears even in bed with nothing else on. When we had sex, sometimes my hair would get caught in its clasp, which hurt a bit and limited my range of motion. I never complained because I could tell it turned him on. Some kind of Tarzan-Jane control thing. Or whatever primitive man it was that used to drag his woman along the ground by her hair. Yes, Paul. Yes I did take my pills. I am fine. But someone is outside our door and I am alone. Please, just tell me when this becomes an emergency.

He's after drugs. For sure. Predators usually are, especially in this neighbourhood. The drugstore down the street has three identical yellow signs in its windows each printed with the message: NARCOTICS SUCH AS OXYCONTIN ARE AVAILABLE BY SPECIAL ORDER ONLY. There is something about the font and the drugstore's logo at the bottom of the signs that make them look polite, almost friendly. And Special Order sounds nice, like the sort of thing picked up by a practical woman in a wool coat, leather gloves and a fine hat.

Hullo, Mrs. Matthews! Your Special Order has arrived.

Oh! Thanks a bunch, Tommy. I'll swing by in the morning.

A brown paper package tied up with string handed over the counter by a smiling pharmacist, like the one in the Norman Rockwell paintings. Toodle-oo, Mrs. Matthews says, the narcotics such as OxyContin tucked under her arm as she waves goodbye to Tommy and the pharmacist with the other gloved hand.

I've heard of this before. A lot, come to think of it. Drug addicts breaking into your house when they know you've got what they need.

Shit.

A bang.

I think he's coming around the side. Narcotics are available in this house, no special order required. The predator must know that. Heard that the missus must be on something good to keep her steady. Damn the big yellow signs! If they weren't taped to the windows he might just be prowling around the alley behind the drugstore, waiting for the right moment to jimmy open the back door with the crowbar hidden in his jacket. But he knows they're available there by Special Order *only*. We all know, thanks to the signs. We all further assume they are locked away in a safe or simply Not On The Premises. Hence, the requirement for special orders.

I didn't notice my heart until now. This makes it real. My heart is pounding so hard I can feel it in my ears. If this wasn't an emergency I wouldn't be feeling this way. Maybe the nature of my emergency will be a heart attack. No matter what, we're approaching the threshold.

Something dropped.

I heard it. Something metal, clanking on the deck. The crowbar. The one he was going to use to break into the drugstore before he saw the signs and resorted to Plan B. This is Plan B. I am Plan B. I'm getting the phone.

It's always good to be prepared for the worst.

It makes you less afraid of life in general, I think.

I always said I'd never overprotect my kids. Or maybe I just thought that. It's hard to remember now. I'd tell them the truth about things, even the sorts of things that are supposed to be beyond them, not meant for children. Like the things my mother would murmur into the phone, dropping her voice and pulling the cord taut around the wall. Where people go when they disappear. What cancer really is. Why grown-ups run away, why they slice into their arms with paring knives and let the blood run from under the bathroom door to soak into the hallway carpet. I wouldn't necessarily bring up these topics, just answer questions as they arose.

That was the plan.

Maybe some weekends we'd walk through streets where sadness lurks. Just to see it, to know it in advance. I could introduce them to homeless people, to street kids especially. Talk about things. All of us, sitting on the sidewalk in a circle with a runaway kid and his mangy German shepherd and his sign that says Every Bit Helps. We'd listen to his story. I would definitely make sure they were not afraid of dogs. Or strangers. Or the dark.

It's ringing.

Ringing. Voicemail, dammit. He must have it on silent. Try again. What hotel is he staying at? Palm Something. It's on my damn cell phone downstairs. This is an emergency. An Emergency. Answer, dammit. Please, Paul. Please.

"Martha?"

"Paul—there's a man. I can hear him—"

"Oh, Martha. I miss her so much tonight."

I can't breathe. Can't form a word.

"Are you in her room, honey?" His voice warbles. I can see his tears, the tiny globes of water that fall straight from his lashes. "Is that where you're calling from?"

"Yes."

"God. Shit. Sometimes I can't bear it."

I lie down, cheek to the floor to feel the cold, staring at the place where her crib had been. Where her bed had been. Where the doll I sewed together from a pattern used to rest on her pillow.

"Martha—"

"Paul. You could have called me."

"I didn't want to upset you. Didn't want to wake you." He takes a deep, wet breath. A web of mucus thickens his throat. "Why are you up, hon?"

"I heard something. But it's gone now."

DREAMS

No one seems to notice the dirty white door when they walk along that stretch of Dundas Street West. Years ago, from the back seat of her mother's car, Carly would have had her eye out for just that sort of thing. The kind of door from which a stormy and unkempt man would emerge, pausing on the step to light a smoke before limping out into the city, a woman tripping onto the sidewalk behind him in a mess of tattoos, bangles, sprayed hair and wild eyes. Carly would have watched them as long as she could, twisting her neck and straining her eyes as they receded from view. Rare to see people so raw, so exposed, reality stripped bare like that.

"Did I tell you," her mother once said on one such ride to Carly's ballet school downtown, "that Ms. Richard sent me a note? Wanted me to know that you're one in a million."

Carly didn't respond. She scanned the passing faces and doors for some jagged shard of life. Her mother had amped up the "special" talk in the months since her father hadn't returned from a business trip for a job he'd never held.

"You hear me back there?" Linda tapped the rear-view mirror with the hand that held her cigarette, smoke from her mouth obstructing her view of Carly. "She said a kid like you comes around once in a lifetime. Think anyone ever said that about me? You're something special, kiddo. Gonna be something special."

"I'm not, Mom," Carly said to the window. "Ms. Richard is a freak."

"Hey—that *freak* was one of the best dancers in the country," her mother yell-talked over her shoulder. "She knows talent when she sees it, and she sees it in you. You think she sends letters to all the parents?"

Trash, the other long-necked girls called her, tittering from the corner of the studio in a shrill fuss of tightly pulled buns. Friends for years, most of them, not there on some poverty scholarship like she was. *White trashhh*, their whispers hissed along the barre to where Carly stood stretching. It felt closer to the truth than anything Ms. Richard said about her.

"You listen to what that lady says, you hear me? To what *I* say. You're gonna be something special."

Carly looks up through the slanting rain to see how close she is to the dirty white door. Home. Recessed between a dollar store pinned with flags and plastic toys, and a Portuguese sports bar flickering with TVs and gesticulating men, it's the boot prints that make it dirty. Impossible to know how many times it's been kicked open from its sticky frame. And the yellow prison-bathroom light overhead doesn't add much to its appeal.

She dips her head down again, fishes her key out of her pocket. A procession of after-work traffic inches its way westward on the road beside her, destined, she imagines, for clean, well-lit homes with white cupboards, red wine, dinner with napkins. She hops up the step to the door, jiggles in her key. She thinks of how she might seem to a girl in a back seat. How thrilling. How real.

She slams her shoulder into the door like a battering ram. It swings open on the first try. A haze of marijuana smoke hovers as she climbs the stairs and slow, throbbing bass pulses from behind the apartment door. Portishead.

Luke and a friend are slouched on the worn couch in front of the television. A joint and a cigarette burn on a plate on the coffee table, bottles of Canadian scattered around.

"Delta One, Delta One. Fire." Luke is in a tank top, his tattooed vine of thorns winding its way up his left arm and across his chest. A cast partially covers the storm-battered ship on his right wrist and hand, broken in a fight weeks ago. He's found a way to play video games despite it—chipping off part of the plaster to fully liberate his thumb—and wears a headset now over his stringy black hair to communicate with his virtual soldiers.

Carly pulls off her wet sweatshirt and goes to the kitchen.

"Hel-*lo*?" he says without turning to her. It's a wonder he can even see the screen; his eyes are practically shut. "Not even gonna say 'hey' when you come in?"

Kian, his friend, juts his chin in her direction. "Hey Carly, lookin' good." He tries to stifle a giggle and descends into silent laughter.

"No gig tonight, I take it?" She twists her wet hair into a bun on the top of her head.

Luke takes a drag of his smoke. "Nah. Not tonight. Tomorrow. Maybe. You?"

Kian can't hold it together and spits out his beer.

She opens the fridge instead of responding. "I thought you were going to pick up some food."

"Did. Table."

There's one slice of pizza left in an open box on a mess of old newspapers, the cheese congealed. She closes the fridge and heads to the bedroom, Luke's cigarette now pinched between his lips as he violently manoeuvres his controller.

"Can you not ash on the carpet?" she snaps.

He pauses the game. Rolls his eyes up at her from under their heavy lids and, in slow motion, ashes the cigarette on the plate. He returns it to his mouth, looks back at the TV and starts the game again.

Carly shuts the door behind her and doesn't bother turning on the light. The glow from the street outside is enough to see the swirl of tie-dyed sheets and crocheted blankets on the bed, the pile of laundry on the floor, the oversized *Taxi Driver* poster taped to the wall. She wriggles out of her damp clothes, tosses them on the pile and slips into her robe. She shivers. She can't call in sick tonight.

Luke's gaze is fixed on the screen as she passes back in front of them, but Kian eyes her up and down without shame. She hurries into the bathroom, locks the door and turns on the shower hot and fast. She wraps her robe tight around her body and sits on the toilet seat, rocking back and forth to get warm. When the room fills with steam, she rolls her shoulders back, hangs her robe on the nail behind the door and bends over to stretch her hamstrings. She looks up just as her reflection disappears in the mirror.

"Travelling Riverside Blues." Almost always starts her set with it now. She had fallen for the slide guitar long ago, and when the drums kicked in, her body still reacted without her brain doing much at all. Besides, she knew that any guy born after 1950 was a sucker for Led Zeppelin. Jimmy Page alone had him in his grip; all she had to do was surrender to the rhythm and play to the lyrics. Regulars had begun to request it, and guys who'd never been there before stopped talking, stopped joking, stopped darting their eyes between the stage and the game on the televisions.

Some nights she can feel the buzz in the club before she's raised from the platform below the stage. She can feel it from the girls who trot back into the dressing room with an added bounce as they count damp bills and roll them into tight wads. She can feel the pole spark with a current as her hair cascades over her face and the DJ above introduces her set like she is the star.

Some nights she's a nymph at a sixties music festival, a girl dancing alone and free in the corner of some bar, and every kick, split, slide and slither is born of the rhythm. Every move and removal in sync with the guitar. Her hair swings loose in thick waves, her lips the sole carrier of expression: full, parted, glossy.

Some nights she has them in a trance. Low, reverent whistles waft across the black room as she slips off her bra and crawls across the stage. Her eyes are mirrors. Her gaze cannot be caught. They throw bills at her and tuck twenties into her G-string. She watches them watching her, their eyes, their lust, more naked than her body as they lean closer, whistling and clapping. They think they can see all of her.

And some nights she feels nothing at all. Eyes all around her fixed up at the game or down at a phone. She spins around the pole, kicks and crawls, and watches girls lead guys to VIP, guessing who will cross the line.

The ones who did said it wasn't much different from what they were doing already. They tucked thick folds of money into their purses at the end of the night. They said it was barely a line to cross at all. She wasn't so sure, she swore she'd never do it, but on a night when she'd drunk and snorted enough and needed the cash, a VIP customer unzipped his pants and the barely there line bled into the carpet with the rest of the stains. He'd caressed her ears the whole time, murmuring over and over that she was such a special thing, such a special, dirty thing, and the barely there line slit open beneath her and she had nothing to reach for as she fell. Afterwards, when he'd opened his wallet and she lit a smoke for something to hold on to, she saw pictures of two young girls who looked just like him, smiling in a portrait studio, light shining in their eyes. He'd snapped the wallet shut when he saw her looking, tossed two fifties on the ground and glared at her with such disgust that she'd cowered, waiting to be struck. Wanting to be struck.

"Scooooores!" Kian cries, releasing his controller and shooting his arms in the air. He runs circles around the couch, nearly smashing into Carly as she leaves the bedroom dressed and perfumed.

"Shit, dude," he says to Luke, plopping back down beside him. "Your girl is smokin'."

Luke looks at her, then back at the screen. Hockey now. He drops his head side to side, cracking his neck as the teams prepare to face off. "It's five–one, numbnuts. I'm still beating your ass."

"Can't believe you let her work as a peeler, man." Kian lights up a freshly rolled joint. "She were my girl, I'd fuckin' never let her leave the house. Lock that shit up."

Luke picks up his friend's controller and holds it out to him, waiting to unpause the game. Unfazed.

"And here I was wondering why you're still single," Carly says into the gap that was Luke's to fill. She looks at his cast as they start the third period, their thumbs bouncing wildly. He'd never told her what the fight was about. She no longer thinks it was over her.

"What time's your shift done?" Luke asks when she opens the door to go.

"Uh, one. I think."

"Taking a cab?" His eyes still on the game.

"Yeah."

"Cool."

The goal horn blares.

"Fuck!" Kian yells.

Luke takes a pull off the joint as the players regroup on the screen. "Call if you need a ride." He gives her a nod. She nods back. She closes the door behind her, stepping lighter down the stairs.

—

Luke walked in on a dead night in January. A quiet month already, the unrelenting snow kept even the hard cores at home. Bars across town were closing early, including the one nearby where his band had been playing, the four of them shuffling in to Dreams with their gear and sinking down into plush chairs at a table by the stage.

The remaining girls ended their sets with glazed eyes and empty hands, slipping back into their robes and flopping on the dressing room couch without bothering to check their makeup in the mirror. Carly took her position, felt the dull rumble as she ascended, closed her eyes and began to move. When she looked out to gauge the room, she saw him watching her. Short black hair, arms sleeved with tattoos, stunned blue eyes refracting the stage light like shattered windshields.

He mouthed something, urgent, as if they shared a secret. She looked away, spun around, tried to blur his face into the rest of the dark. He stood up. She dropped to all fours. She saw a regular at the door stamping snow off his boots. She crawled toward him. She caught her breath. But before she got far she felt a hand slip a bill in her thong. She felt a face by her face, a mouth by her ear, whispering, *Look at me.*

"Look at me," her mother said again.

"I don't want to."

"I want you to see what they did."

"No, Ma, I don't want to."

"All right, all right. I'm not going to torture you, little bugger." Linda pulled her sweater back down again. "You can open your eyes. I'm all covered up."

Carly held their dinner plates. Fried hamburgers on the stove. At fourteen years old, it was the best thing she knew how to make.

"Welcome home, Ma." She put the plates down on the TV trays in front of the couch, squirted an extra dollop of ketchup for each of them.

"Mag-ni-fi-co! Home cooked. Beats the hell out of hospital gruel." Linda clapped her hands but sounded beaten, her voice low and shaky. "Now, tell me about Cinderella. I wanna know all about your solo."

A month before, Carly had come home from rehearsal to find her mother sitting on the couch with the television off. Linda sat still for a moment before stubbing out her cigarette in the glass ashtray and ironing out the folds in her robe with the palms of her hands. She looked directly at her daughter and opened her mouth as if to say some-thing then closed it again. After a minute she lit another cigarette, pulled up her feet and reached for the remote.

When Carly brought in the plates later that evening, she had to wait longer than usual for her mother to put out her smoke and sit up. In fact, her mother didn't move at all and kept staring at the television even though Carly was blocking her view.

"Mom? Dinner."

"Cancer."

"What?"

"I've got cancer."

"What are you talking about?"

"They said they have to take one, then do chemo."

"What? What do you mean?"

"They're going to take my right breast and then I'm going to get chemotherapy."

Carly tried hard not to drop the plates. She tried to focus on a hole in the wall where a picture of their family had hung, all three of them dressed up for Halloween. Superheroes. She'd been Wonder Woman.

"Don't worry, kiddo," her mother had said, sitting straight and tapping out her cigarette. "They said they'll make me a new one, nicer than the one I have now." Her laugh rattled with phlegm and turned into a cough. She saw the shock in her daughter's face. She held up a hand until her hacking subsided, then said, finally, softly, "I'm not going anywhere, babydoll. Nowhere. You're stuck with me. Okay?"

In the end, they took both, but it didn't matter. She was gone in nine months.

Look at me.

It was a plea. Carly balked, yanked her head away and slid back up the pole, his smell of smoke, Irish Spring, mint, whisky lingering in her nostrils. She looked at him, through him, spent the remainder of her set staring away from his eyes, trying to control the rhythm of her breathing, her heartbeat.

"Look. At. Me," Ms. Richard repeated, tapping her hand on top of the piano in time to the music. "Look! At! Me!"

Carly pirouetted across the studio, sweat stinging her eyes as she forced herself to look at her teacher. She lost her balance and slipped for the fourth time.

"Again." Ms. Richard twirled her finger in the air. "*Focus.* Let me see your eyes. Let me see you. Let me see what is happening *inside.*"

The piano accompanist started again. Carly shook her head to regroup, tried to steady her ankles as she stepped back into position.

"You once swallowed this whole," Ms. Richard said.

"I'm sorry." Carly awaited her cue, chin high and tilted, quivering on her toes, arms raised in an arc. "I'll try again."

"Listen to me. You made this your own, you reinterpreted something I thought I knew inside and out. Take me back there. Let us back in."

Carly swept her long arms down, her feet left the ground, she was in flight. A mechanical bird.

"Look at *me*!" Ms. Richard bellowed over the piano and clapped her hands to get Carly's attention. "Let us feel your anger."

Carly missed a step. Her right leg gave way as if turned to water. The pianist halted with a cacophonic tinkle.

"Again."

But Carly did not get up. Her breath heaving, she stared at a scratch on the studio floor.

"Up. Again!" Ms. Richard cried, louder than before, amplifying the tremor of doubt she'd managed to quiet all afternoon. "You are on the cusp."

She went to her, grabbed hold of her arm to lift her up. Carly wouldn't stand. Her arm flopped down.

"Carly—"

"I'm tired." She stared at the scratch, her teacher's shoes in the periphery. She could dam the tears as long as she didn't move, as long as she stared at the scratch. She could not bear what would break through. She knew it would sweep her away.

"Carly."

It was not like Ms. Richard to relent. Her shoes stayed in view, scuffed, old leather worn where the knots on her feet threatened to bust through. They stayed long after she had excused the pianist with a curt nod, long after she'd considered and rejected all possible phrases of encouragement, long after her protégé had lain down on the floor.

It was dark when Carly awoke. A sweater folded beneath her head, a jacket blanketing her curled body. The studio door left open just enough to let in light from the hallway. No one was there, though, when she went to it, when she let herself out into the night.

Jerry, the manager, poked his head around the corner and met her eyes in the mirror.

"Shift's almost over," she said before he could say anything.

"Well, they want you. Place is dead. Get up there."

He was at the table alone. Arms crossed against his chest, he watched her walk slow, sparkling with body dust under the violet lights, to where he sat.

She leaned over him, grasping the arms of his chair. The performance had begun. "Did you want a dance, baby?"

He nodded. His eyes wouldn't drop from her face.

"Come," she said, breathier this time, and started toward a room in the corner, shifting her weight slowly from one hip to the other so he would be distracted by her body. His hand brushed hers and her left knee buckled and she felt like a fawn just learning to walk.

Inside the red room she closed the door behind him and crawled up on the table. He slid onto the black vinyl couch. She turned so her ass was in his face. She straightened her legs and rolled her body up.

"I think you're remarkable," he said as she stepped onto the couch and stood over him like an Amazon.

"Mmm." She sunk to her knees, straddling his lap.

"I want to take you out."

She took off her bra and let her head fall back so he couldn't see her eyes as he touched her. His fingertips grazed her nipples. For a flash, she let herself pretend they'd been to a show, to dinner, that they were now back at his apartment. Then she turned it off and pressed her crotch into him. Two minutes left in the song. She could count it down. When he reached up to touch her face she rose higher so his hand landed on her breast instead.

When it was over he got up and took out his wallet. He pulled out two more twenties and a business card and dropped them on the table. "My number's on here. My name is Luke. And I'm pretty sure you're the most beautiful girl I've ever seen."

He looked at her once more before walking out, the door clicking shut behind him.

She heard Lindsey singing in the hallway and shoved the card under her makeup bag just as the dressing room door swung open.

"If you get caught doing blow in here, Jerry'll kill you." Lindsey flopped into a chair as she twirled her long hair into a topknot and whistled into the mirror. "Got a warning last week."

"I don't do that shit anymore."

"I saw you hide something under your kit. I'll take it if you don't want it."

"Jesus—I don't have any blow."

"Well, let me know if you find someone who does. I could use a bump tonight." She took a swig from a lip-stick-smeared wineglass, lit a smoke, smudged her already smudged black eyeliner with an expert pinky finger. "That guy you danced for? Holy Mary. He was fucken hot. Did you suck his dick?"

"Yeah, Linds. I did. And all his friends too."

"Did you see how he was looking at you? Like, *looking* looking." She whistled low and less musically this time. "I'd be all over that ass—"

"Trix," Jerry said from the door. "You're wanted."

"Tell me something I don't know." She stubbed out her smoke in the overflowing ashtray, reapplied her sparkling red lip gloss and squeezed Carly's boob on her way out. "You're pretty hot yourself, love." She sang from the hallway, "I'd fuck you too if you'd let me."

The squeeze of her hand lingered for minutes after she was gone. Bass from the music upstairs rattled the mirrors rhythmically like a giant pumping heart was going to bust through from behind. Blood and shards of glass everywhere. April and Lisa, the only other girls in there, sat side by side on the couch in the corner, heads moving to a slower beat as they listened to a track off shared earphones. It was midnight. Carly's shift was over. She pulled on her leggings, her boots, her coat and jammed the card in her pocket.

In the hall, she motioned to Jerry that she'd be leaving out the back. He tucked his magazine under his arm and followed her to the dented steel door. She kicked it near the bottom where it always got stuck, and slammed her hip into the bar.

"Got it?" he asked, leaning behind her to hold it open.

A gust of snow whirled in.

"Yeah. See ya tomorrow, Jer."

He looked down the alley in both directions. She trudged through the snow and heard the door slam shut when she reached the safety of the empty street.

"Hey."

She looked up, eyes wide, ready to bolt. A silhouette flicked its cigarette and stepped toward her, into the light.

"Hey," she said, bracing herself.

"I'm not crazy," Luke said.

"Okay," she said, still bracing herself.

"I was just thinking, nights like this, they're, like, once a year? When you can walk down the middle of Bloor Street and not see a car for, like, miles. Snow everywhere."

She didn't say anything.

"Okay, well . . ." He stepped toward her, gingerly, with one hand out, as he would to a wounded wild animal. "I just. I thought you might want to walk, for a bit."

—

It's still raining when she gets out of the cab after her shift. A laughing couple under an umbrella bump into her as they scurry past, the apology in the girl's eyes curdling to scorn when she gets a good look at Carly.

"She's totally a ripper," the guy says, sneering over his

shoulder. She slides the key into her lock. He eyes her, proprietary. She kicks the door with her boot.

At the top of the stairs, the sporadic strum of a guitar. One chord disconnected from the next, hands, fingers blindly searching for some never-heard melody. Luke's on the edge of the couch when she steps inside, leaning over the coffee table, trying to write notes with his left hand. He sits up again, strumming with a pick, singing quietly about a bird with a broken wing.

"Ah yes," she says, pulling off her rain boots. "Those broken-winged birds are always the most beautiful, aren't they? Nothing like a broken bird to heal, a flightless bird to make your very own. Forever obliged."

She pours a glass of wine from the open bottle on the kitchen counter. He takes a cigarette out of the pack in front of him, taps down the tobacco and lights it, staring at the wall.

She sips her wine. She waits for his retort. There is always a retort.

He looks at the table.

Her pulse quickens.

He stands, cigarette between his lips as he lays his guitar in its case, the notepad in his beaten leather satchel.

Before she can double-down he says, "Your father died. Your brother called, to tell you."

He slings his guitar case on his back, the satchel over his other shoulder and goes to the bedroom. Drawers opening and closing. "I've been thinking of how to tell you for the past few hours."

He comes out again, stuffing clothes into his bag. "But I'm not sure why I bothered. Nothing gets to you, right? Hard as a fucking rock."

He's at the door before she can form a word. He says the number is on the table. His shoes clapping down the stairs before she can move.

When the door to the street slams she runs, barefoot, after him. Down the stairs, onto the sidewalk. She dives back for the doorknob before it locks behind her. She doesn't have her key.

"Luke!" she yells, leaning out into the rain, eyes wide down the sidewalk in one direction, then the other.

A passing pack of bar-hoppers gawks at her. University kids. "Fuckin' trash!" one of the guys bellows, hidden among the chuckling others. A girl turns, looks in wonder.

Carly sprints back up the stairs for her boots and her keys. But when she is out front again, she has no idea which way to go.

His wobbly left-handed block letters sketch the name, the number on a ripped envelope on the kitchen table. An area code she doesn't recognize. She dials.

"Hello?" The voice groggy, muffled.

"Is this Troy? I'm sorry, I didn't think—"

"Is this Carly?" He tells her to hold on. Whispers to someone. The rustle of sheets or clothes, the click of a door. "Carly? I'm so happy you called."

His voice is shaking. He is in Salt Lake City. He is younger than her. Married. In sales. A baby girl. He apologizes for being so nervous. "Dad talked about you at the end. He wasn't too with it then, I didn't even think you were real."

"Dad."

"Dad, yeah. I'm sorry—this must be so weird."

He exhales to let it settle. She stands in the middle of her living room. Rain against the window.

"He said you were a dancer? Said he used to watch you. Figured you were pro now, or must be pro now. It took me a while to track you down."

The fridge whirs to life. Her own breath in the earpiece. He swallows into her quiet.

"Sorry," he says. "Wow. This is harder than I thought it'd be."

"Has he been there? In Salt Lake? I mean, is that where you were born?"

"Born and raised, yeah. He and my mom, they met here."

"So he's been there, in Salt Lake City, this whole time?"

Troy sounds like he's holding his breath. He lets it out. "For the most part, yeah."

She listens to the rain with eyes closed. She could be anyone, anywhere. She tries to pretend she is someone, somewhere else to trick the riot raging to life inside her. To hold it back.

He clears his throat. "They—well, Mom now, she lives not too far from here. She thinks you should come."

Carly lets out a sound, a beat of a laugh. "Did he know that mine died?"

He says nothing for a moment. "I'm so sorry to hear."

Rain getting harder now. She opens her eyes to watch it blur the window. Blood pounding in her ears like a fetal ultrasound.

"Listen," he says. "This is obviously a lot for you. Why don't we try—"

"When. When did he watch me? You said he watched me dance."

He swallows again. "I don't know. Nothing was too clear by then. But listen, I want to say that I think he was sorry. I think that's what he meant, when he was talking about you."

She makes the sound again, the rest of the laugh escaping.

"This isn't easy for me either," he says. "To not know about you, to go my whole life."

Her breath feels like black smoke when she exhales. It fills the room. The rain beating against the window, she can hear through to its rhythm now.

"Does that matter?" he says.

She's listening hard. There's always a rhythm. It isn't easy for everyone to hear, but Carly can always hear the rhythm. Her riot stomping, clanging in time. Her head bobs, catching the beat.

POSTCARDS

JANUARY 5

I know, it's been a while. Eight months? Nine? Longer, I guess. Africa this time. Ghana. Not yet sure when I'm coming back home.

I had this memory yesterday, one of those flashbulbs. It came to me when I was sitting on a bus stuck in a crowded market. Heat pressing in, an angry voice bleating over the radio. People everywhere around us. Women with babies on their backs and loads on their heads, oranges, papayas, bananas, cassava. Men pushing carts, pulling wagons, piling tilapia onto tables. Drivers yelling out of duct-taped taxi windows and leaning on their horns. I exhaled hard out of my nose against the stench of sweating bodies and decomposing fish, and motioned out my window to a young girl with a bowl of water sachets on her head. She turned only her eyes to me as she shuffled over so the bowl would stay level, and had to step quickly to keep up when the bus started to move. I reached out to trade her a coin for some water and then it all just fell away—the girl, the market, the hot vinyl seat under my thighs—and I was on the beach in Cape Cod.

My father is setting up the camera on a tripod. He's swearing at it, first because he can't get it to lock into place, and then because he can't remember how to set the timer so we're all in the shot at once. It's November, the only month he can get time off work, and curse words from the blend of languages he's picked up at the factory mix with his terse Ukrainian.

Cape Cod, of all places. Such misfits here. My mother loved the Kennedys, Jackie in particular, and that's why we've come; a wood-panelled motel room tight with extra cots is to be our version of the Kennedy Compound for five days. I'd been sullen and silent for most of the ten-hour drive along the darkening highway, furious they'd stolen me from my friends, angrier still at my mother's delusions.

Our first family walk through Provincetown: wide-eyed caution as we head toward the sea. Quaint and colourless like other seaside towns when the months bend to winter, it only winks here and there at the life that fills its streets in August—washed-out blue cottages boarded up for the season, a tattered rainbow flag limp above the drugstore, faded All Night Party posters lacquered to a brick wall, a leather outlet with mannequins still armed with whips in the windows.

I know Mother has realized this isn't the Hyannis Port of her black-and-white *Life* magazine dreams, but she acts like it doesn't matter as she consults the brochure she's taken from the motel and points to the sites as we pass:

"There's the Lobster Pot."

"Here's the library with the sailboat on the second floor . . . should be open tomorrow."

"Oh! Here's a passageway that leads to the ocean."

My father's steel-grey eyes take in the rest as he marches along beside her, tripod gripped in his immense right hand that is warped and hardened from decades of twisting wrenches, the fraying camera strap slung over his rigid shoulder.

He isn't an easy tourist. His walk is stiff, his eyes suspicious as he presses his palm into my mother's back, directing her past two men smoking by the drugstore who are cackling like aged beauty queens. For once, he doesn't shout at my young brother and sister for shrieking and dallying behind us. I take Sasha and Ava by the hand and follow my parents through the walkway to the beach.

"We should take a picture here while the tide is out," Mother calls over the waves. She points to the rotting pier behind her. We arrange ourselves, shivering against the wind—her hands on Sasha's shoulders, his eyes on the ground, Ava's face stretched into a clenched-jaw grimace (the only way she, at five, responds to cameras), my gangly arms crossed over my chest—as my father fiddles with the camera and tripod a short distance away. His curses mingle with the wind, waves and the whistle of blowing grass. Finally, he walks over, still grumbling, and stands like a soldier by my mother.

Flash.

Then another,
and another.

And I was back in the bus on the torn vinyl seat, bouncing along a broken road, smelling tilapia grilled whole on the street. My fellow passengers looked out the windows or fanned themselves, their calm and patience discordant with the outrage of the man on the crackling radio. My chance at water was gone but it didn't matter much because I was almost home.

Home.

The last two pictures used to make my mother and me laugh. In one, we're all heading in opposite directions as my father strides toward the camera, loosened. The other is a close-up of him, blurry, nearly right up his nostrils. I don't remember that one as much because he tore it up when he saw it. He probably would have torn up the other, but Mother hid it behind her when we first got them back from Black's, and kept it in her drawer buried beneath her rolled-up socks and folded nylons.

The first photograph, the one he meant to take, where he stands erect and unsmiling just apart from the rest of us—Mother framed it and put it on the table with the porcelain lamp in our living room. It's the one they put in the paper.

JANUARY 16

I need to tell you that I've forgotten winter. It hasn't been that long, but the heat here is so thick and unrelenting, I'm barely out of the tub before I'm dripping again. Sweat rolls down my body, one drop in a race with the next, while I wait on the road for a taxi. My clothes are always wet.

I remember this Blake poem about winter that I had to read in high school. Not the verses so much, but how it made me feel. The ice and snow and groaning rocks, the bleakness, the cruelty of the season. Stark open space and raw winds that scrape against your skin. I could see the tiny silhouette of a man in the empty blowing white, wondered where he could be going.

Last night I drank wine on a friend's balcony overlooking rusted tin roofs and the river his poorest neighbours squat in to shit. You wouldn't believe the roar of the rain when it pelts against those rooftops; the thunder, when it comes, is no match for that steady, deafening drum. The wine we drank was cheap and sweet, and the bottle perspired in the heat of the evening. He said something about not missing winters at home in Germany (or Austria?) and it made me think of that poem. And then of Sasha.

Sasha in his sled. He is young, maybe two. I pull him behind me in our snowy yard at night, our shadows long in the light slanting from the bedroom windows. I race along the fence with the sled's handle in my grip, kicking up snow and taking care to avoid the corner where my father's tomatoes will grow in the spring. Sasha throws his head back and laughs puffs of warm breath into the cold, clapping his woollen mittens together soundlessly. As soundless, almost, as the snowflakes drifting,

drifting,

to rest all around.

Blake conjures this now. Sasha laughing in the face of a soulless winter, gripping the sides of the sled with his too-big mittens.

The German was asking if I wanted a cigarette. I told him there were things I missed about winter. He said we weren't talking about that anymore.

JANUARY 30

In the market today I bought avocados and pineapple from the thin woman in the shapeless green dress. Every week now I'm there, buying fruit from her stand. She's not sure if I'm here to stay or if I'll disappear when the thrill wears off, like all the others who bought a ticket for this ride. At least, that's how I interpret her indifference. She counts my money without stopping her conversation with the other women who sit on the bench and look out at the road, tsk-ing and shaking their heads.

This morning, for the first time, she looked me in the eye when she told me how much I owed her, and as I pulled the bills from my pocket, trying to think of something to say in return, I felt this hand on my arm. A woman's hand, a mother's hand. I knew without even turning to look. My bra strap must have slipped down my arm because she was tucking it back under my sleeve, squeezing my shoulder as if to keep it in place. I swivelled around expecting to see a warm maternal smile, but instead she was stern, her face etched out of rock, cold brown eyes circled with blue. She was different from the other women in the market with her black leather purse and navy suit and blouse. A government worker maybe, or a lawyer. She held the hand of a little girl in a school uniform and backpack who watched me with the same hard stare while her mother led her away.

My mother looks at me from the other end of the front hall. She's by the door, the covered basket of eggs and braided bread beside her, ready to be blessed by the priest. She steps into her brown leather church shoes and turns to the mirror to tie a scarf around her head. I always told her that the scarf made her look old, but it really made her look like a starlet from the sixties, ready for a jaunt in a convertible.

Photos never did capture her as I saw her. At the mirror, knotting the scarf under her chin, running Revlon Red lipstick over her mouth. Any moment now she'll call to Sasha and Ava demanding they be at the door in an instant. Worn down by months of resistance, she no longer forces me to go, and is silent as my siblings race each other toward her. She hooks her arm under the basket handle and follows them out to the car, sending a ripple of guilt to my core.

I had to ask the woman at the fruit stand to repeat how much I owed her, which made her kiss her teeth before saying again forty thousand. She nodded at me as she took the bills and met my eyes once more before I turned to leave.

People here go to church for four hours on Sunday mornings. Four hours. The preachers shout and sing through blown speakers, women fan themselves with cardboard and dance in the aisles with tambourines. Everyone goes. I was thinking I might, one Sunday. I don't know. It just seems like a long time to be stuck with God.

FEBRUARY 12

I met this girl Karen from England. She works with the UN at the refugee camp an hour from the city where we live. It's not like the ones you see in the news—there aren't flapping tents or emaciated children lying immobile on makeshift cots. This one was a hospital complex long before the first Liberian civil war. It's now a place where thousands of Liberians live, some for more than fifteen years, some for their whole young lives. There are stores, schools, a newspaper, community meetings. Men gather around radios listening to the BBC World Service, arcing and adjusting the antennas to get reception, and launching into heated political debates. Boys play soccer between the sky-blue huts that are stencilled with black numbers.

I've gone with Karen a few times now and have become friends with one of the writers for the camp newspaper. Leonard is his name. He's lived there for almost ten years and used to be a radio host in Monrovia. Music and politics, he told me, as if they always went together.

He sings a cappella with a group formed at the camp and today he played me a tape of their songs. No instruments, he said, we came here with only our voices, so that is how we do. He rewound the tape at one point, listened closely, and said they had to work on their harmony in that number. I asked if he lived here with his family. We were sitting outside, on the steps of a small medical building overlooking a sun-baked field. Teenaged boys were playing soccer, torn rags of blue or red tied to their arms to indicate which team they were on. Leonard watched, his eyes darting to keep up with the rapid shifts in the game.

Two sisters, he said. But there had been nine of them, nine siblings. Four sisters, four brothers, plus his mother and father. He might still have brothers in Liberia. Two of them were shot with his father, his mother and two sisters raped and stabbed in the back room.

It is hard to say, he said. Hard to say.

I see them all in their final movements. Mom stirs soup in her striped yellow apron. Ava and Sasha, cross-legged, play *Super Mario Bros.* in the basement on the worn shag carpet. Sasha's nails bitten down to nothing, Ava's painted sparkly purple from when I'd visited the weekend before. My father loads his rifle in the cement work room beside where they play. Or maybe it's loaded already—of that, I'm never clear.

He doesn't need it for them anyway, not for the little ones, his huge hands enough for their thin necks. My mother must have heard something because she's at the doorway when he comes upstairs and he gets her in the chest and the forehead, the wooden spoon still in her hand when she slumps to the ground. Then, in the quiet, he makes it to his brown plaid chair where the barrel clinks against his teeth.

We sat and listened to Leonard's music and watched the match until I had to go home.

FEBRUARY 27

Buses idle in front of the camp in plumes of diesel smoke, waiting to take refugees back to Liberia. Voluntary repatriation. Families queue in the black haze with large plaid shopping bags packed with the things they've amassed since living here. The men yell and chase away European and North American ex-pats who pretend they're not there to take artistic pictures.

I talked to Leonard today about going home. He said he wanted to, but didn't know when and didn't know what it would be when he got there. He asked when I was going home. I pretended I didn't hear the question.

Sometimes Ava's the clearest. I wish she wasn't. Eyes like my mother, white-blond hair soft like dove feathers. She runs to me where I wait by the fence after school to pick her up. She doesn't know I've been there long enough to see her stand up to the bossy girls. Fearless in that schoolyard. On our way home, she walks with her hand in mine and I tell her that I think she's brave.

Brave like you? she asks.

That afternoon she swings around the uneven bars in gymnastics class as though her body has no weight and the ground beneath is made of Jell-O, while I watch from a bench at the side.

I don't so much anymore, but I used to wonder if he thought of me when he did it. If he had an image of me at my desk, while he slipped the bullets into his rifle, sitting in my dorm room, staring at the bookshelf. *Molecular Biology, Fourth Edition, Complex Analysis, Principles of Physical Chemistry*. If he could picture how my pen rolled onto the floor and down the vent as he walked up behind Sasha and Ava, how the metal lamp singed my arm when I lunged for it. How I searched in vain through my drawers for another pen as he went up the stairs to the kitchen, to my mother, how I laid my head down on my notebook for a rest as she collapsed to the floor. How I woke with a start, with a stiff neck and dents on my cheek when my roommate burst in with her boyfriend.

Well, by then it didn't matter.

I see him, though.

He storms out of the house, looking for his wrench, and finds it in my six-year-old hands trying to take the training wheels off my bike. He snatches it away and crouches down beside me on the driveway to remove the bolts with slow, enormous hands. He doesn't tell me to go away but carries on, pretending he isn't showing me how to do it. His hands were big, but never slow. Not like that.

When the wheels are off, he holds the bike steady at the handlebars and with a quick nod signals for me to get on. It takes three tries but I am off, wobbly, riding away, down the black asphalt and onto the sidewalk.

When I turn to come back at the corner, I pretend I can't see him watching me.

I'm going north tomorrow.

Or maybe east. Or west.

Or maybe I'll wait to go with Leonard to see what's left in Liberia.

THE DATE

I'll know you when I see you

Doreen typed to Sean, despite the mask he wore in his profile picture.

I feel like I know you already. :)

She hit Enter.

She watched the clock in the corner of her computer screen.

8:23.

8:24.

8:25.

Saturday then? he responded.

She exhaled.

Paused.

Then typed Saturday then into the message box, appending a ! then deleting it, afraid she'd already betrayed too much giddiness with the smiley face. She didn't want him to think her desperate and childish.

And she did, somehow, know it was him when he stepped into the restaurant and shook the rain off his yellow umbrella. The colour was like an electric middle finger to the drab greys of the November suits and overcoats that shifted and sighed on bar stools with their backs to the door. Her wineglass clicked against her teeth. She wanted to bite through and crunch the glistening shards between her molars, grind them up, taste the blood, anything to keep her looking calm and cool on the outside.

As Sean shook his umbrella dry, the yellow caught the eyes of diners who turned to see and didn't turn away. *There's something about that guy*, she could hear them thinking. *A real spark.* She'd known it. Known it the first time they Clinked. The restaurant's host gave Sean a warm slap on the shoulder. He was clearly a regular, which thrilled Doreen even more as the place was new, expensive and had a signless alleyway entrance. Sean chatted with the host as he slipped his umbrella into the stand and handed over his well-tailored coat. He yanked his cap firmly down onto his forehead—he'd not be giving it up. Doreen locked her jaw to keep from eating the glass as the host led Sean to her table.

"Doreen?" His shadow hovered above her.

"Sean! I knew I'd know it was you! Remember how I said? As soon as you came in, I was like, 'That's him!' So." Her hand trembled as she took another sip.

Sean ironed his magenta tie flat as he sat down and tucked his chair close to the table. He was saying *apologies* and *taxi* and *the office* and *King Street a mess*, but she didn't quite hear it all.

"Sure. This time of day," she managed. She concentrated

on placing her glass back down so it wouldn't fall from her hand and smash to bits on the reclaimed barnwood floor.

Take the edge off and *great cocktails here* and *try something new for a change*, he said as he picked up the drinks list, scanning it with his small, wide-apart eyes. He held it up in the casual way a celebrity might, someone in the habit of blocking unwanted attention, but permitted Doreen an unhindered view of his features. Such as they were. Now that candlelight blotted away the shadow that had fallen from his hat, Doreen saw that Sean did not have a face.

"You've got to try Clink," Gretchen had said three weeks earlier, when she and Faisel came home to find a sodden Doreen sitting on the floor in the dark living room, swigging whisky sours. "Remember Alma? That's how she met Harvey. Or Marvin. Whatever his name is." Gretchen lit a joint and opened the balcony door a crack. "Look at them now!"

Alma from the office who was pregnant with twins. Alma who had been proposed to at the company Christmas party, Harvey sweating through his suit jacket and stumbling over a taped-down power cord on his way to sing a cappella at the lectern, a crumpled speech in his hand. Everyone cried.

"Hm." Doreen threw back the rest of her drink and pressed her eyes shut as Faisel flicked on the light. She'd finished the pinot grigio in the fridge and found only rum and whisky in the cupboard, but the former made her think of

Cuba where she and Connor were supposed to go for their honeymoon, before he'd left her for his business partner.

She's, I don't know, happy, Connor had said when he broke it off, his face in his hands so he couldn't see Doreen writhing on the ornamental rug. *It's like, what you see is what you get.*

Happy? Happy!? What does that even mean? Happy. No one is 'happy' all the time.

That's not true. She meditates.

"Everyone meets online now, Dor," Gretchen said, blowing a spectre of blue smoke out the balcony door. "It's not like it was. That's how *we* hooked up." She nodded over at Faisel, who'd been texting since they came in. He worked in film or television, his thumbs dancing ceaselessly on his iPhone.

"It's true," he said without looking up. "I've heard good things about Clink."

Doreen knew he'd say anything to get her out of Gretchen's condo, where she'd been staying since her breakup.

"Seriously. A guy I work with is on it," he went on. "He's a good guy, like, not at all trash. Just divorced is all." He went over to Gretchen to take a pull off her joint, then continued, holding in the smoke. "Or maybe his wife died. Cancer or something. Anyway, good guy." His phone chirped. He smiled at whatever was on his screen and exhaled into the living room.

Sean tapped his menu and said to the waiter, "Steak frites. Don't even know why I bother looking. Creature of habit."

Clink cost five hundred dollars to join, so Doreen had

figured the people on it were serious. Or rich. She saw a preview of some of the men and they were nice-looking. They had white smiles. They had jobs in offices and weren't drunk or overly tanned or in Cancún in their profile pictures. It had taken her almost two hours to fill out the questionnaire, and at the end of it, after a brief processing pause, the algorithm spat out the first of her six matches.

Sean.

He was holding a carved wooden mask over his face, backdropped by lush green foliage.

"And for you?" the waiter asked.

It was a hobby, Sean had told her the first time they talked on the phone. Seeking out isolated populations around the world. It started when he was young, when his family skipped from continent to continent with his father, a mining engineer. *Sounds like an expensive hobby*, she'd said. He'd laughed, thoughtfully. Almost apologetically. *More like a labour of love, I guess.*

"Miss?"

Where Sean's nose and cheeks should have been his skin was stretched taut, his mouth a lipless slit, his eyes two watery black beads. He held a neatly folded napkin to his chin as he sipped his ice water, careful to catch what dribbled from the corners of his mouth. He looked out the window at the lashing rain. His profile a plane of skin.

"Perhaps you'd be interested in our catch tonight," the waiter was saying. "Mahi-mahi, flown in from Hawaii this morning. The chef has prepared it with a coulis of—"

"Sure," Doreen said, shoving her menu at him. "Could you tell me where the washroom is?"

She was trying not to gag. She wanted to bolt. She wanted her money back. She wanted to pound Gretchen and Faisel into the ground with her fists.

A bottle of champagne arrived before she could get up.

"This is from Jasmine," the host said as he placed two flutes on the table. "The owner," he explained hastily to Doreen. "For our esteemed guest this evening." He smiled at Sean as he untwisted the muselet and draped a white napkin over the cork to catch it as it popped. He poured their two glasses and left the bottle in a silver bucket in a stand beside them, nodding deferentially at Sean as he departed.

"Cheers," said Sean, tilting his flute toward Doreen. "It's great to finally meet you in person." He waited a few beats to see if she would lift her glass, then tapped it with his anyway. "Well. *Salut.*"

He dabbed his chin with his napkin. "Okay. Well, I've managed to compress this to a few sentences."

She stared at the tiny rising bubbles in her glass, her mouth hanging open a crack.

"I was fourteen," he said. "Living in Zambia. I'd been in an argument with my stepmother—she'd 'accidentally' let my pet monkey escape that morning. I took off on my bike and pedalled for miles to the site where my dad was working. I was going to tell him I was moving back to Canada to live with my mother. I'd heard she was in Calgary somewhere. I sped along the dirt roads, weaving around the potholes, thinking of what I would pack—my camera, baseball cards, the few things that came with me everywhere. I rode right past the security gates and spotted my father's blue hard hat on the other side of a big pit. And that's the last thing I saw." He paused, turning the stem of his glass. "They said later they'd let me through the gates because of who my father was. Chief engineer of explosives. They didn't want to lose their jobs." He lifted his flute. "Anyway, twenty years and twenty-four surgeries later, here we are," he said, clinking their glasses again. He didn't wait for her this time and took a swig, napkin at his chin. He nodded when Doreen excused herself to go to the washroom.

As soon as she slid the lock into the stall door, she texted Gretchen.

Today 7:38pm
Help! He's a freak! He doesn't
have a face!!!

Today 7:40pm
WHAT!??

Today 7:40pm
NO. FACE. Some kind of explosion.
Hence mask in picture.

Today 7:41pm
Your lying!!!

Today 7:41pm
No!!! Need to get out of here.
In bathroom but no escape window

Today 7:42pm
Hello???

Today 7:44pm
HELLO???!! This is YOUR FAULT

Today 7:46pm
Sorry!! Faisel called . . .
don't leave! Think of the story
you can tell after!! Its just dinner.
You dont have to fuck him.

Today 7:47pm
;P

Today 7:47pm
Ahhhhh! Going to puke!

Today 7:48pm
Seriously!!! HELP ME.

Today 7:50pm
Faisel agrees. Don't go.

Today 7:50pm
ALSO—I know your not a mean
person!! Cant judge a book by
its cover etc.

Today 7:51pm
Fuck. FUCK!! Okay. Just dinner.
But that's it. and I want my
money back!!!

Doreen washed her hands and went back into the restaurant, pausing at the bathroom door. Sean was looking out at the rain with his hands folded, barely moving, the two glasses of champagne on the table in front of him. His singular loneliness was unfathomable to her. She inhaled and went back to her chair.

"Sorry, I . . ." She realized she hadn't come up with an excuse for why she'd been gone so long. "A friend called. She needed my help."

He pressed his mouth slits together. "Is everything okay?"

"Yeah." She smoothed her napkin over her lap. "Wasn't an emergency or anything." She winced and took a sip of champagne.

"I'm just glad you decided to come back," he said as a waiter set their plates in front of them. "That doesn't always happen."

The host brought over a bottle of red wine and turned the label toward Sean. "Our sommelier says this is exquisite with the steak, Mr. Roche. It's a '93 first-growth Bordeaux.

New to our cellar." He poured a small amount in a glass to taste. "He's available if you have any questions."

Sean swished it around his mouth and nodded his approval. The host filled their glasses and backed gallantly away.

"So what's the deal?" Doreen asked. "You some kind of movie star or something?"

Sean took a small bite of steak and had a sip of wine, patting his mouth with his napkin as he swallowed. "My business had its IPO this week. It went better than expected."

"Oh?" She looked from her plate to the rain outside. If she squinted to make things blurry and concentrated on seeing him with only her peripheral vision, he could look almost normal.

"Just an Internet thing. Behind-the-scenes programming. I won't bore you with the nerdy details." He said he wanted to talk about her instead, the places she'd travelled. "Weren't you recently in Greece?"

She'd put it in her Clink profile (*List any recent travel destinations*_____) but not that she'd gone the night Connor had ended it with her. Not how she'd grabbed her purse, her passport, and left their home in a cyclone of tears and smashed wineglasses and a desperation to scratch off her own skin. She'd hailed a taxi on the street, violent winds chucking her hair all over, and shook the whole way to the airport. There was a seat open on a flight to Athens. She'd charged it to Connor's Visa. *No, no bags to check.* The woman at the desk looked at her suspiciously but handed over her boarding pass anyway. She would buy all that she needed when she arrived. A bathing suit. Underwear. Strappy sandals and a loose flowing dress and big sunglasses and a wide-brimmed straw hat. Once she was in the air, drinking her second mini chardonnay, she was soothed by thoughts of stark white buildings against a blue sky and sea. This postcard vista, all she knew of Greece, was so clear and cool and uncluttered. She was convinced it would calm the simmering fury and mend the pulpy remains of her heart as she sat on a balcony with wine and cheese and olives. Salt air flowing in and out of her lungs. She'd smiled as she pictured it. She would be cleansed. Purified. Renewed. Healed.

But then she arrived and the streets were in chaos. She watched a man set himself on fire in the middle of a public square.

"I went to see the Acropolis," she said. "The history there, and all."

"Sure," he said, nodding. "I get that."

"What about you? You never said where you were in that picture. The one in your profile."

"Madagascar," he said. He told her about a tribe there, where, years ago, babies began to die. "The people thought they'd done something to offend the spirits," he said. "One mother lost three in a row and when her fourth was born, she cut marks into his face to make him ugly, so the spirits wouldn't take him away."

"Jesus. It didn't work, did it?"

"Well, he didn't die, if that's what you mean." He speared three frites with his fork and dipped the ends in aioli. "All the mothers started to do it, so the elders made it a ceremony. They would carve a mask out of bark before each baby was born and the mother would take it and cut the same design into her newborn's face. Each mask a different pattern. Kind of like a snowflake. They made one for me."

Doreen shook her head. "It's barbaric."

"Maybe," Sean said, pouring more wine for them both. "But when I got there, there were all these beautiful teenagers walking around with faded markings on their faces. Like the most magnificent tattoos. It would have taken your breath away."

She liked how he'd included her in that, how she could have been there too. They sat quietly for a moment, sipping their wine and looking out the window. A woman ran past in high-heeled boots, head down as though that would keep her dry, her hair already a slick river down her slender back. Sean watched until she dipped into her car and drove away.

Anyone would look beautiful running in the rain, Doreen wanted to say. She wanted to go outside, jog back and forth in front of the window to demonstrate.

"So they all lived, then?" she asked.

"Hm?"

"You said there were all these people with scarred faces. It must have worked, then."

He swirled his wine. "No. Lots of babies died. So, no, I guess it didn't."

"Oh my God! Doreen!" Gretchen pounced on her when she was barely through the door. "That was fucking amazing. I'm just like, wow. *Wow.*"

Doreen leaned Sean's dripping yellow umbrella against the wall. He'd given it to her at the end of the night when they realized someone had taken hers. Easy to mistake, black like the rest. She was tingly from the champagne and wine, the cognac that had come with dessert.

"Gretch. I'm exhausted," she said, taking off her shoes. "I promise I'll tell you all about it tomorrow."

"You should see the comments!" Gretchen grabbed her hand and pulled her to the coffee table where a laptop was flipped open, the only source of light in the room. "You felt something, didn't you? Don't lie! Don't lie to me. This is fucking amazing. I'm almost, like, *I can't believe you're standing right here!*"

On the screen, a man was being interviewed by a sprightly young woman with a swoosh of white-blond hair. She was leaning over the arm of her chair as if she couldn't get close enough to him.

"So he gave her the umbrella," the woman said. "That was just so sweet!"

"Yeah. It was a very authentic gesture. I mean, we're thrilled."

"I'll say! Did you honestly think this could happen?"

He smiled, shaking his head. "This went way beyond. Way beyond our expectations."

Tweets scrolled along the screen below them.

@stacey325: SEAN has the #humantouch! Mind blown!!

@starlightbrite: Professor! YOU ARE A GOD! #humantouch

@zach_bibleraiders: Doreen gives us all hope!! #humantouch

"Professor McGivney, let's go back to the part just before dessert when SEAN talked about the children he'd seen in that 'tribe'—priceless, by the way. It was like that all really happened. And the whole bit about the Internet IPO? I mean, come on. Those details! You're really amazing!"

He waved away her praise. "Can't take credit. SEAN's conversation program was developed by Abe Matumbe, a postgrad in my lab. He's a genius with nuance."

"Don't be modest!" the pixie woman said, playfully slapping his leg. "Okay—here, check it out . . ."

A screen popped up within the screen, and there was Doreen sitting at the dinner table, looking directly into the camera. Her eyes moist, her lips and teeth stained greyish purple with wine. She was smiling sadly, visibly touched by something she'd heard.

Doreen sunk onto the couch. "What . . . what is this?"

"Shhh!" Gretchen plopped down beside her. "You have to see what happens next!"

Doreen on the screen shook her head almost imperceptibly, staring into their eyes.

"Gretchen . . ." Doreen whispered. "What is going on?"

"Shhh!"

A tear appeared at the corner of screen-Doreen's eye, mingled with her mascara and fell from her lashes in a perfect sphere. Then another. She wiped her face, smudging black along her cheekbone.

The man and pixie woman came back into fullscreen, the woman dabbing her eyes with a tissue. "'I mean, wow. That was just so beautiful. Am I right?" She turned to the camera and applauded, as if encouraging a live studio audience. Then back to the man, "Did you think you could make it happen so fast?"

"I think she's been going through a lot. Maybe on another day, under other circumstances—"

"Let's be clear here—we *know* she's not an actor or anything. We've all read her profile. Why do you think SEAN could make her feel like that?"

He shook his head, at a loss. "It really is so much richer an experience than we ever expected. He's programmed to pick up on certain signals from people, which he uses to determine whether what he's talking about is engaging or not. But, in all honesty, we're just amazed."

Doreen appeared again, smiling, then laughing. She'd never seen herself like that before. How different from her image in the mirror. Her face so much looser, one eye slightly bigger than the other, emphasized by her laugh, which was crooked. She was both uglier and prettier than she thought. She cringed at the double chin that appeared when she looked really happy. Doreen on the screen kept laughing, wine spilling over the edge of the glass in her hand. She was someone she didn't recognize.

"Wait!" the pixie woman cried, touching her ear. "My producer is saying she's back. Faisel—bring her up!"

The living room brightened in a flash of white. Doreen blinked hard. When she opened her eyes she saw herself squinting on the screen, haggard under the harsh lights. Makeup smudged, hair flattened by the rain, eyes red and puffy.

"Doreen! Whew! What a night!" the pixie woman said from a smaller rectangle. "I know this must be kind of overwhelming, but you were selected from a huge pool of great ladies for ZTV's *The Human Touch*. This has been an incredibly moving experience for all of us. Thank you. Thank you so much!" She turned to the man, flapping her hands by her face. "Oh my God! I'm going to start crying again!"

Doreen's ears were ringing. Gretchen had snuck away and was now a silhouette on the balcony, cell phone at her ear, her orange cigarette light zigzagging like a firefly in a Mason jar.

"You've stolen our hearts, Doreen! Not to mention SEAN's!"

Doreen covered her face with her hands. "Can someone please tell me what's going on here?"

"What?" Pixie woman leaned closer to the camera. "Faisel—can you bring up her audio? I'm not getting any . . ." She paused, holding her ear, nodding. "Okay, we've got a little technical glitch. While we get that sorted it'll give me a chance to introduce Doreen to Professor Oren McGivney. Chief robotics engineer and cognitive scientist from MIT's Artificial Intelligence Lab. Did I get that right? I guess we can kind of call you SEAN's dad, huh?"

The man laughed. "Not quite. I have a great team." He looked into the camera. "Hi, Doreen. I know this must be a lot to take in."

Another screen popped up, B-roll of people in lab coats standing around Sean, who sat inanimately in a chair. One of them took out Sean's eye, inserted a small screwdriver and turned it delicately.

The living room shifted. Doreen clawed at the fabric of the couch.

The pixie woman said, "Can I break it down for her, Professor?"

"By all means."

"Here's the long and short of it. You and a few other very special ladies were chosen for *The Human Touch*, an online reality show that tests the behavioural believability of the most advanced versions of AI. And just how do we do that? By seeing if they're able to make someone like you fall in love with them!"

"Let me interject here, if I may?" Professor McGivney asked.

"Of course!"

The professor leaned forward. "Doreen, no one's been able to make a human-looking face for an artificial being that doesn't—for lack of a better term—*creep* people out. It has to do with something called 'the uncanny valley.' So my team decided to create someone without a face at all."

"And so far—he's got the Human Touch! Sorry to interrupt, Professor, but this is really just so exciting."

"Not at all."

Doreen closed her eyes, concentrated on her breathing. "I'm on drugs. Someone drugged me. That's what this is."

"Oh! We can hear you now! You're adorable. No—no drugs! Maybe we should back up a bit." Pixie lady looked over at the professor and smiled. "Clink? The dating site? Totally made up. Your profile was so perfect. You hit all the markers of being completely average."

There was a knock. Doreen looked at the door.

"Now Doreen—" Professor McGivney said. "We don't have that much time here. Understand that SEAN is a next-generation BioBotic. He's made with a mechanism that allows him to develop 'real' feelings and attachments."

"If I can cut in here, Professor—" pixie lady said. "Doreen, you were so . . . I don't know. What's the word? Authentic? Human? Alive? In any case, that little *je ne sais quoi* of yours really seemed to bring something out in him. In all of us watching, am I right?" She stood and clapped, nodding and looking beyond the camera, then sat back down. "So, congratulations—you guys are going on to the next round!"

Doreen looked up. "Sorry, this is a game? I'm in a game?"

"Wellll, yes and no. It's a competition, and it's also real life. But it's up to you to decide just how real you want it to get." She winked.

The knocking got harder, more persistent. A voice from the other side of the door: "Doreen?"

"Oh my gosh! Is that him already?" Pixie lady flew back in her chair. "Wow, Professor, he found the place pretty fast."

"He'd have no trouble tracking her with his internal map, and the chip she swallowed at dinner."

"Decisions, decisions! What a night you've got ahead

of you, Doreen!" the pixie woman said. "While you were gone, our team of stylists transformed your room into a super-romantic boudoir."

Another window popped open, panning a red room that flickered with scores of candles, the bed dressed in ruby satin sheets.

"Now before you decide what to do," Professor McGivney cautioned, "I should tell you he's been developed to be an *exquisite* lover—"

"Yes, Professor, let's talk about his endurance. Wait till you hear this, Doreen!"

The professor removed his glasses and cleaned them with his shirt. "Let's just say we've tried to make him as human as possible in just about every other capacity but this one. He's kind of a superman in bed."

"Whew!" Pixie woman fanned herself with both hands. "You are one lucky lady!"

The knocking got harder. "Doreen? Can you open the door? Please. Don't listen to them."

"And I'm not just talking about how long he can last," the professor said. "His physicality. It's a little out of proportion."

"Doreen, I think you're going to get some stiff competition for SEAN's affections. Take a look at the comments on Twitter now!"

@pjgarnerXTC: OPEN THE DOOR GIRLFRIEND! If you don't want his #humantouch, I DO!!!

@renattaspinata: Just turn out the lights and go wild! Give me some of THAT #humantouch!!

"Doreen? Seriously. Open up."

"No pressure, Doreen. Either way," the professor said. "Either way we learn something."

Doreen looked out at the balcony, Gretchen's silhouette against the charcoal sky.

"Maybe she should go check out the room?" the pixie lady said. "See how it's been all tricked out? The rose petals? The sheets? I bet that might nudge her in a particular direction." She winked again at the camera.

"Doreen?! Turn that off!" the voice yelled from behind the door. "Don't listen to them. It's not true. I was burned! I can tell you all the details. Zambia, my father, the hard hat. For fuck's sake. Please, Doreen, this is ridiculous. I'm real! Just open up."

The only other way out was through the balcony door, twenty-three floors above the expressway.

"Doreen—please. I can explain this. None of it is true."

Gretchen tossed her cigarette over the glass railing, the glowing spot of orange arcing up, then disappearing. Smoke streamed from her nostrils.

Doreen slammed the laptop shut. She yanked out the cords for the lights. She slid the balcony door wide open.

Gretchen's smile faded. "Hey," she said, backing up.

Doreen's breath caught in the wind. She got up close and pushed Gretchen against the railing.

"What the fuck is wrong with you?" Gretchen yelled. "Stop! What are you doing, you crazy bitch?"

Doreen started to cry. She pushed Gretchen once in the chest, hard, then went back inside, locking the door behind her. She followed the streak of light coming in from beneath the front door, and paused for only a breath before unlatching the deadbolt.

MOONMAN

When the sky turned black I thought of my father. But that makes no difference to you now. *Where were you when it happened?* you ask, and I say that I was at work, in my cubicle, in the centre of the city. Which is not untrue. Hunched over my keyboard, the computers blinked off with a defeated drone, the lights flickered out, and the silence of a city cut from its power rose up from the ground.

A quiet more unnerving than darkness, just like Moonman had whispered.

How did you get out? you ask, meaning methods, vehicles, escape routes. You want to hear about the path you assume I took west to the wide roads and stiff stalks of corn, whether I knew about the tunnels in advance, etc., so you can amend your own plans of now-constant preparedness, mental networks fizzing as they rewire.

I don't tell you that when the black clouds rolled across the sky I didn't go anywhere and my first thought was of the man least capable of protecting me from the end of the world.

———

I saw him the way he was, with a mug of red wine and a pack of Player's Light on the other side of the screen door that led to our small backyard. He could sit out there for hours on summer evenings, smoke lingering around his head in varying densities like a dirty halo. He sat and smoked, looking out, facing elsewhere, while Mom dried the plates and glasses with a blue dishtowel, then went upstairs to put Alice to bed.

I'd sometimes pretend he was out on that step listening to a Jays game on the radio, unwinding after work like dads at the time had a tendency to do. I imagined that if I opened the squeaky screen door, he'd shift over to make a spot for me and he'd tell me that there were two out at the top of the fourth with a runner on first and third. We'd sit just listening for a while, and when the game began to drag he'd talk about stats and trades and the players he watched when he was my age, and near the bottom of the seventh, when the score was 4–2, he'd tell me to fetch our gloves from the garage so we could throw the ball around until it was time for bed.

Instead, on most nights after dinner, I was inside lying on the rug in front of the TV, and he was out there alone on the back step, wishing he were somewhere else.

I was ten when he came home on a Saturday afternoon with a used guitar. He ruffled my hair as he crossed the front porch where I was colouring with Alice, his fingertips leaving trails on my scalp like swaths cut through a wheat field. I followed him inside and watched as he leaned the banged-up guitar case against the couch. He got himself a glass from the cabinet and whistled on his way to the kitchen where he rummaged through a high cupboard, clinking bottles together until he found what he was looking for. I'd never heard him whistle. He returned, his glass half-filled with a nectar like dark honey, and stopped when he saw me, his lips still pursed in melody.

"Hey Simon," he said. "Wanna hear something, little man?"

I nodded and moved closer as he set his glass down on the coffee table. He brought the case onto his lap, clacked open its locks and lifted the lid to reveal a plush red interior cradling a scratched black guitar. He ran his fingers along its strings before pulling it out and nestling it against his torso. Then he tuned it, his eyes closed and head cocked as though listening for some secret. And when he started to strum, a whole different man took the place of my father.

Something dropped on the floor in the upstairs bathroom. A second later my mother was there on the stairs, her hair pulled back with a bandana, yellow latex gloves on her hands glistening with water.

It was just before Christmas when he left his job at his uncle's car dealership. My mother wore a hood of silence as she peeled carrots and potatoes over the sink, her dark hair hanging forward like a curtain so none of us could see her face.

"Molly, you're not even trying to understand," my father said. He leaned against the counter beside her with his arms crossed tight over his broad chest, his eyes cast down at the tile he kept poking with his big toe. She peeled harder and faster until the carrot in her hand looked more like a weapon than a vegetable.

"Babe," he said, "come on. You think it was easy for me to make this decision?"

As though he wasn't there at all, she chopped up the potatoes and carrots, dumped them in a pot of water and set it on the stove. She grabbed plates and cutlery from the shelves and drawers, set the table for three, then opened the oven door to check on the meat.

"It's pork," she said, slamming it shut. "Dinner will be ready in an hour." She wiped her hands on a dishtowel, tossed it onto the counter and didn't say anything to Alice and me on her way through the living room and up the stairs.

"I'm getting really tired of this martyr shit!" Dad yelled to the ceiling as he went out back, the screen door clattering against its frame.

Alice and I sat like statues on the living room rug in front of *Wheel of Fortune*. I thought that if we didn't move, if we didn't say anything, we could blend into the furniture. I was relieved when he came in a few minutes later and went upstairs.

"Big money! Big money!" Alice called out and clapped her hands.

I elbowed her in the ribs. "Shhhh!"

The bass of voices in their bedroom got louder and

louder until something whumped hard against the wall, rattling the trinkets in the cabinet beside me.

Footsteps in the hallway above. Fast but not running, my mother came down the stairs, my father close behind.

"Molly, wait," he called to her. But she was already out the front door. Because I didn't hear the creak of the porch steps, I knew she hadn't gone far and imagined her leaning over the railing, which, in a way, was just as bad.

That spring I turned eleven and got a bike for my birthday. By then my father wrote music during the day and played Bowie cover songs in bars a couple nights a week, and my mother worked the overnight shift at the radio station where she was a producer. I'd heard her on the phone with someone not long before she started working nights, saying that Alice and I wouldn't even know that she was gone, that she'd be around for bedtime and back home to take us to school in the morning.

"My aunt is staying over the nights that both Chris and I are out," she said into the receiver. "I don't know, Fran. It's going to be tough, but I think it's only temporary. I mean, my hours and his . . . *situation*." And then she laughed in that conspiratorial way that mothers share when talking about husbands and children. A laugh, it seemed to me, that rarely reflected joy.

I couldn't tell her that she'd been wrong. It didn't matter that she was home when we went to bed and when we got up in the morning, her nighttime absence echoed through the halls. We always knew when she was gone. I lost the feeling that children are supposed to have when they drift off to sleep: the knowledge that their parents, their mother, is in the house somewhere, her protective warmth flowing from room to room in the dark. Without it, I lay awake for hours listening to every creak, every rustle and every snore that rose up from Great-Aunt Audrey, who slipped into an impenetrable slumber on a chair in front of the television minutes after the key turned in the lock.

In search of a direct line to my mother, I brought up the old brown clock radio from the basement one night, plugged it in by my bed and tuned it to her station. I knew I wouldn't hear her voice, but it didn't matter. I could imagine her in the windowless studio I'd visited on a PD day, sitting at the control board pressing buttons, adjusting dials, directing the show in silence. The studio felt as serious as an operating room and everything in it seemed important, including my mother, without whom I believed the whole thing would fall apart.

I crawled under the covers with the radio and slowly increased the volume.

"They know more then they'll ever let on while they ply us with television and hamburgers and the Super Bowl, pounding our brains into a doughy pulp. You can't hear them but they're laughing. Right now. Laughing at us."

The voice stopped. A man's voice, almost whispering. I felt like I'd caught him in the middle of telling a secret. I waited a few seconds before reaching for the tuner, thinking maybe I had the wrong sta—

"*Laughing!*" he boomed, the radio tumbling from my hands and clunking to the floor. Aunt Audrey's snore broke into fits before returning to its sinusoidal cadence. I picked it back up and pulled the blanket over my head.

The voice was whispering again. "Laughing. At us. And you can bet your last ounce of gold that they'll be laughing harder as they watch us try to peeeeeeel our flabby bodies off the couch when it comes time to fight back."

Pause.

"To fight the New World Order."

Pause.

"If, that is, we ever open our eyes to what is happening. To what—really—is happening."

Longer pause.

"I'm Moonman and this is *The Age* on the Striker Radio Network."

I burrowed deeper to where it was hardest to breathe and decided that when Moonman came back from commercial, I'd focus on the silence between his words. It wasn't hard to do. I knew if I listened hard enough, that I could hear my mother in that silence, that I could hear her breathing. She was always there in the soundlessness. Quiet on the board signalling to Moonman to break, quiet in the kitchen packing our lunches for school, quiet with Alice asleep in her arms through the crack of the bedroom door.

I tuned in to Moonman under my blankets every night she was gone. I listened to him talk about the Illuminati, about life in other galaxies, about Area 51 and what really happened to JFK. I learned about the symbols of the New

World Order, the secret histories of world leaders and the imminent End of the World As We Know It. Moonman knew more than anyone I'd ever met, and every night I felt like he was sharing secrets of the universe with me alone.

If I wanted to, I could blame him for what happened. I could say that he planted seeds of curiosity about the world at night, that he inspired me to explore the dark, that listening to him made me feel intelligent and brave and old enough to creep down the stairs past sleeping Aunt Audrey, into the garage and out onto the street with my bicycle.

But, really, I think it was rage that sparked it. Rage or insomnia or just the plain white terror of being left alone in the dark. Or some of all three.

I rode off into the starless city night, pedalling hard and fast, cutting through streets and laneways toward the main road. Darkness rustled the leaves high overhead and I was breathless with adrenaline and the metallic taste of the night air that in no way resembled that of the day. I knew where my dad was. He'd pointed it out to me one afternoon when he picked me up from school—the pub where he played his music.

I had to blink against the bright street lights when I turned onto the main road, standing up as I pedalled along the wide sidewalk, zipping past people out for a nighttime stroll or huddled in dark doorways smoking cigarettes.

"Hey—kid!" someone yelled. "Little late for a bike ride!"

I slowed down and rode close to the storefronts as I approached the pub, slipping into the shadows of the awnings that lined the way. I heard music. A man's voice singing something familiar. *Chris Coates tonight 9 p.m.*, written in pink chalk on a sandwich board outside. I hopped off my bike and leaned it against the window of the shop next door. When I was sure no one had seen me, I crouched down beside the planter box in front of the pub and peeked into the window.

He was right there, sitting on a stool with his back to the street. His feet were perched on the lowest rung, his heels bouncing up and down, keeping time. A column of sweat soaked through his shirt along his spine. On the small stage floor beside him was a bottle of red wine and a half-empty glass, and everything was hued pink and green by the lights cast from the ceiling above. My father strummed his guitar while he sang hard and loud into the microphone. Even through the glass I could hear that his guitar sounded more alive and desperate than it ever had in our living room.

I looked past him into the pub where candles pocked the dark like grimy stars. A group of college kids were making their way to the pool table at the back, the girls stirring candy-coloured drinks with tiny straws. Two men in plaid shirts drank beer and ate nuts at the bar while they watched hockey on televisions hung from the ceiling, and three young women sipped white wine and looked around the room without talking to each other. One couple sat facing my dad, a blond woman leaning back into the man she was with, a number of shot glasses and beer bottles on the table beside them. The man seemed to be having a hard time keeping his head from bobbing around. The woman was staring at my father. When the man said something in her ear, she swatted at his face with long fingers and didn't take her eyes off the stage. I looked around for others listening the same way, but outside of a few people nodding to the music now and then, no one else seemed to be paying much attention.

When he stopped playing, the blond woman was the first to clap. She sat up straight and pressed her elbows against either side of her chest. A few others turned to applaud as well, but none as vigorously as she did. I heard my dad say something about taking a break and I dropped down as he slid off his stool.

I looked one last time and saw him standing in front of the stage, pouring more wine into his glass. He was talking to the woman. She smiled with big white teeth and tossed her blond hair when she laughed. The man she'd been sitting with had fallen asleep with his chin on his chest and was being nudged, hard, by a chubby waitress as she cleared their empty bottles into a black dish tub. Dad walked to the bar, the woman chatting close beside him. He smiled at her in a way that was moist and young, a smile that bared too many teeth and a hunger I couldn't recognize.

I rode home. Fast. The wind felt colder, harsher, like it was scratching at my throat with sharp fingernails. I was suddenly very tired and I wanted my bed. My radio, my blankets. My mother's inaudible breaths in Moonman's pauses. I stood on my pedals and pumped hard, turning from one street to the next in wide arcs. A block from my house, I took a corner too quickly.

I remember headlights.

Nauseous in the aluminum lighting.

Thick throbbing in my ears.

Mom and Dad shadows cut out against a white ceiling. Alice's singsong voice at the end of a long, warbling tunnel.

Can't talk. Can't move.

Nurses checking tubes and dials, stroking my forehead, looking down from far up, into my eyes. A dull faraway inescapable pain.

Dad somewhere in the room with his guitar once. Or always.

Mom hovering in the quiet spaces between.

I left the hospital near the end of autumn. The surgeon came down to see me on my last day. He tousled my hair and told me to buy a lottery ticket on the way home. When my mother wheeled me through the front door I knew right away that our house was not the same: a new emptiness in the hallway, the coat rack gone, the spider plant no longer trickling its spindly leaves from a stand by the stairs. I was lifted ("Careful! Careful, everyone, the scar on his back still hasn't healed . . .") to a hospital bed wrapped in *Star Wars* sheets in the middle of the living room. The television that had been on a console against the opposite wall was now on a chair by my bed between stacks of comic books and bouquets of helium balloons. The couches and arm-chairs had been pushed to the dining room, the table itself nowhere to be seen. New drapes had been hung on the big window overlooking the porch and the street, silky sheaths that let the sunlight in while hiding me from curious neigh-bours; my experience of the outside world, in turn, reduced to dreamy, shimmery snatches of ordinary life.

There were pictures missing from the hallway. For days I stared at an edge of wallpaper that was lifting near the railing, trying to remember which one had been there.

A steady stream of assistants paraded through the door, nurses and therapists checking scars, lifting arms, bending legs, taking measurements. ("He's progressing well, Mrs. Coates. Kids have a tendency to bounce back.") I asked for a radio. Mom was always home now, but on wide-awake nights, when everyone was sleeping, I still listened to Moonman in the dark.

Since he was usually swept up in the current of nurses and therapists and caregivers, it took a while before I real-ized that my father didn't live with us anymore. Huddled under a blanket on the porch one afternoon, still feeling achy and watery from an infection, I watched my parents talking by my dad's parked car across the road. Mom crossed her arms over her chest and looked past him far down the street. He fiddled with the keys in his fingers. She said something and nodded a few times before heading back up to the house.

He opened the car door and was about to get in when he looked up at me. I pretended I couldn't see him.

Drugged, groggy, it wasn't hard to stare out at nothing. My mother came up the steps and with the back of her soft hand touched my forehead, then my cheek, and kissed me before going inside, the door banging shut behind her.

"See ya in a bit, soldier," my father called out.

"Oh," I said, acting like I had just realized he was there. I lifted my arm, held up my hand. "Okay."

He slid into the driver's seat and unrolled his window. The radio blared. He flicked it off and lit a cigarette. For a moment he sat there and then drove off with his hand out to catch the wind.

My mother married Stephen when I was fourteen. Their ceremony quiet, silvery, cozy with night. He was a gentle but faraway man, a serious look in his pale eyes behind the small round glasses that he was always adjusting. His long, thin hair was tied in a ponytail that curled down his back, grey wisps framing his bony equine face. When he moved in, he brought heavy boxes filled with books, two lamps, a pair of jeans and three black T-shirts. He bought a globe at a garage sale to show me how countries were drawn in the decades before the First World War. He touched my mother whenever he could.

One evening on the porch when he was writing notes, I asked him if what he talked about on the radio was true. Without looking up, he said he didn't know what truth meant anymore. I liked when he responded that way.

"I mean, are those things really happening?" I asked.

"Some of them already have," he said, consulting one of the open books on the table beside him.

"But I mean, the really bad things, like the end-of-the-world kind of stuff."

"It's cyclical, Simon," he said. He removed his glasses and rubbed his eyes. His voice bent in the direction of his on-air delivery. "And it's relative. There's a rhythm and a plan. Most is beyond our control."

"But I mean—"

"Simon," he said, looking straight at me. "Are you asking if I believe there will be change, even significant change, in our lifetime?" He held his breath and held my gaze as though expecting some deeper understanding to reveal itself in my eyes, some realization I would come to that would prevent him from having to say what he really thought. But I was long accustomed to his pauses by then and thrilled to be his private audience for what felt like a particularly omniscient insight. I leaned toward him, blinking.

After a moment, he released a lungful of sour air.

"Yes," he said, returning to his books and jotting down a note. "I do."

—

You call and tell me how you remember the salespeople and middle managers and secretaries and vice-vice-presidents chatting about weekend plans as they descended the windowless concrete silos of office building stairwells, cell phones in leather holsters, name tags swinging from lanyards around their necks. *All the sheep*, you say, but not without pity. You gave them a quick smile of reassurance because that's all you could do as you and everyone else poured out onto the sidewalk. The grid of city streets locked with idling cars, drivers leaning out of their windows, squinting at the horizon, nearly decapitated by bicyclists whizzing past. Everyone with phones to their ears, looking east, then south, then west, then north, then at the useless phone in their hand as one network went down, then the next, then the next, and then all we had left were the people in front of us, people slowly being covered in ash and soot that fell from the sky like black snow.

It was so much like how Moonman said it would be. He'd warned us. He hoped that we'd fight back in time enough to prevent it from happening, that we'd Wake Up and See Through the Lies, the attempts to tranquillize us. But his was only a voice in the night. And half the time, when you were tuned in, listening under the covers, it was impossible to tell if you weren't just dreaming.

On spring and summer weekends, Stephen rose early and drew a map of the garage sales in the neighbourhood that had been advertised on handmade signs taped to lampposts, charting the most efficient course from one to the next and home again. He rarely returned with anything. He said to me once that buried treasure was hard to find.

On winter weekends, he sat in the worn wingback chair that he had dragged to the living room window, flicking the newspaper from page to page, raging under his breath at our collective blindness in the hazy, dusty light.

Now he's on an island with my mother. I think. I like to think. Somewhere where an evening sun glistens orange and gold off the sea as they sit watching it on a mat she wove from palms, her head on his shoulder. Alice in a tree house nearby yelling "Big money! Big money!" at an old TV set that washed up to shore.

My father went back to the car dealership to pay for my treatment that the government wouldn't cover, and moved into an apartment above a drugstore nearby. He set up a bench press by the living room couch, his guitar in its case in the bedroom corner where it remained partially hidden by an Ikea wardrobe. When I went to visit him, he'd chain my wheelchair to the bike post out front and carry me up the two long flights to his door, holding my chest close to his. He took each step slowly. We didn't speak as he ascended, so the journey felt long. I once broke the quiet by telling him that he didn't have to be so careful, that I wasn't made of glass, but he still went slow. Another time, during my grade twelve exams, I was exhausted and let my head drop on his shoulder, nearly drifting off as we went up and up and up. I heard his heart beating faster, and sounds of broken breathing. When he sat me down on the plaid chair, he said he was going to order a deluxe pizza and went over to the phone on the wall with tears in his eyes.

I'd like to think he's on an island somewhere too, playing Bowie songs to a ragtag commune of tanned and shaggy octogenarians who listen and bob their heads as they sip hooch out of coconuts. But I can't picture it, as much as I want to. He was the first person I thought about when the ash clouds rolled over, but I'm still not sure if it was because I wanted him to save me or if it was the other way around.

My producer, Cal, says the lines are already lit up. He says we're on in two. I glance up at the old digital clock counting down on the wall of the studio, then return to highlighting my notes and stacking them in three piles. Hour one, hour two, hour three. All twelve lines on the phone are blinking in front of me.

Cal stands at the control board with his left hand on the fader, the fingers of his right hand counting down in silence.

Five. Four. Three.

Two.

One.

My theme song comes up. It's a song my father wrote a long time ago. It's not even that good, but it's been shared millions of times since I started playing it off the top of the show. I let it play for a while, then click on my mic.

"It's Wednesday," I say, pausing as the music comes up again. "We're all still here," I say. "For now."

You tune in from all over to find out how to survive. You think I've got the answer. You say I'm the only voice you can really trust now, and you whisper it over the line as if I'm the only one who can hear you, as if the quiet dark around you isn't rustling with perked-up ears. You think

I'm genetically predisposed to outlive everything so you buy my duplicate genes by the ounce and inject them into your veins, not even waiting for the zone nurse to come around and help. You press your radio to your ear to hear what I will say next and panic when the signal is lost. You know but do not care that as we rebuild our cities, our countries, our continent, I've built an empire on you.

You do not know that when the sky went black I went nowhere. That the elevators stopped working and I watched everyone cluster to the windows then file toward the stairs, looking at me sympathetically as they passed. Someone will be up soon, they said, squeezing my shoulder. You do not know that I was alone in the dark when my phone rang and it was my mother telling me in a low, quavering voice to go into the washroom and lock the door. She said she had Alice. She said don't worry, just go. Then the network went down and that was that.

I don't tell you that I didn't make it out that day. I don't say that I rolled my chair into the washroom and breathed in recycled air and drank toilet water in the blackness, the blankness, of the days or weeks that followed. I don't tell you that I was rescued by a man in a makeshift haz-mat suit who was pulling the building apart for wires and copper and wood. I don't tell you that I was nearly dead. You don't even know that I can't walk. That is no way for a hero to be.

I've told you elaborately concocted tales that even I believe half the time. I run through them again in my mind before I say, "Let's go to the phones."

Cal says, "Chris is on line one."

"Chris," I say, "welcome to *The Seed*."

"Simon," he says.

I don't say anything. No one knows my real name.

"Simon," he says. "It's me."

My finger hovers over the drop button on the phone. I push it.

ACKNOWLEDGEMENTS

Thank you to Kiara Kent, whose passion for the collection and preternatural gifts as an editor lifted each of these stories (and me) to a higher place. To Melanie Tutino and Shaun Oakey for their hawk eyes and surgical red pens, and to Martha Kanya-Forstner, Amy Black and Kristin Cochrane for their enthusiasm from the start.

To my agent Martha Webb for her years of patience and support as progress on this book was stalled by day-job demands and the birth of children. To said children for inspiration that far outmeasures the interruption. To Mary Sirk, Harlene Jeffrey, and Mike and Kelly Meehan, who care for said children (and me) so I can do this. To Mike Jr and Emily Meehan for the encouragement. To Jillian Thorp Shepherd, Stephanie Matteis, Tara Marshall and Raizel Robin for their honest reads on this and everything else. To the lingering influence of John Vervaeke, Asli Gocer and Beth Kaplan, and to writer RS Croft whose stories about being a dancer stuck to the bones and partially inspired "Dreams". To Dave Richards for his mentorship, and for championing my work along the way.

And to Daniel. None of this, without you. (In the best way.) Of all the stories I know, ours is my favourite. My love and gratitude, always.